Poet, performer, anthologist and
born in Guyana in 1949 and ca
Grace Nichols in 1977. His coll
to Pan, I Din do Nuttin', Mango
Light Travel Dark and *Border Zone.* John Agard's awards include the Casa de las Americas Prize (Cuba), the 1997 Paul Hamlyn Award for Poetry, the Cholmondeley Award in 2004 and the Queen's Gold Medal for Poetry in 2012. In 2021, John Agard was the first poet to be awarded the BookTrust Lifetime Achievement Award. *Inspector Dreadlock Holmes and Other Stories* is his first collection of fiction for adults.

INSPECTOR DREADLOCK HOLMES AND OTHER STORIES

JOHN AGARD

HopeRoad Publishing
PO Box 55544
Exhibition Road
London SW7 2DB
www.hoperoadpublishing.com
@hoperoadpublish

First published in Great Britain in 2022 by Small Axes
an imprint of HopeRoad

A CIP catalogue record for this book is available from the British Library

Print ISBN: 978-1-913109-87-5
E-book ISBN: 978-1-913109-93-6
Printed and bound by Clays Ltd Elcograf S.p.A

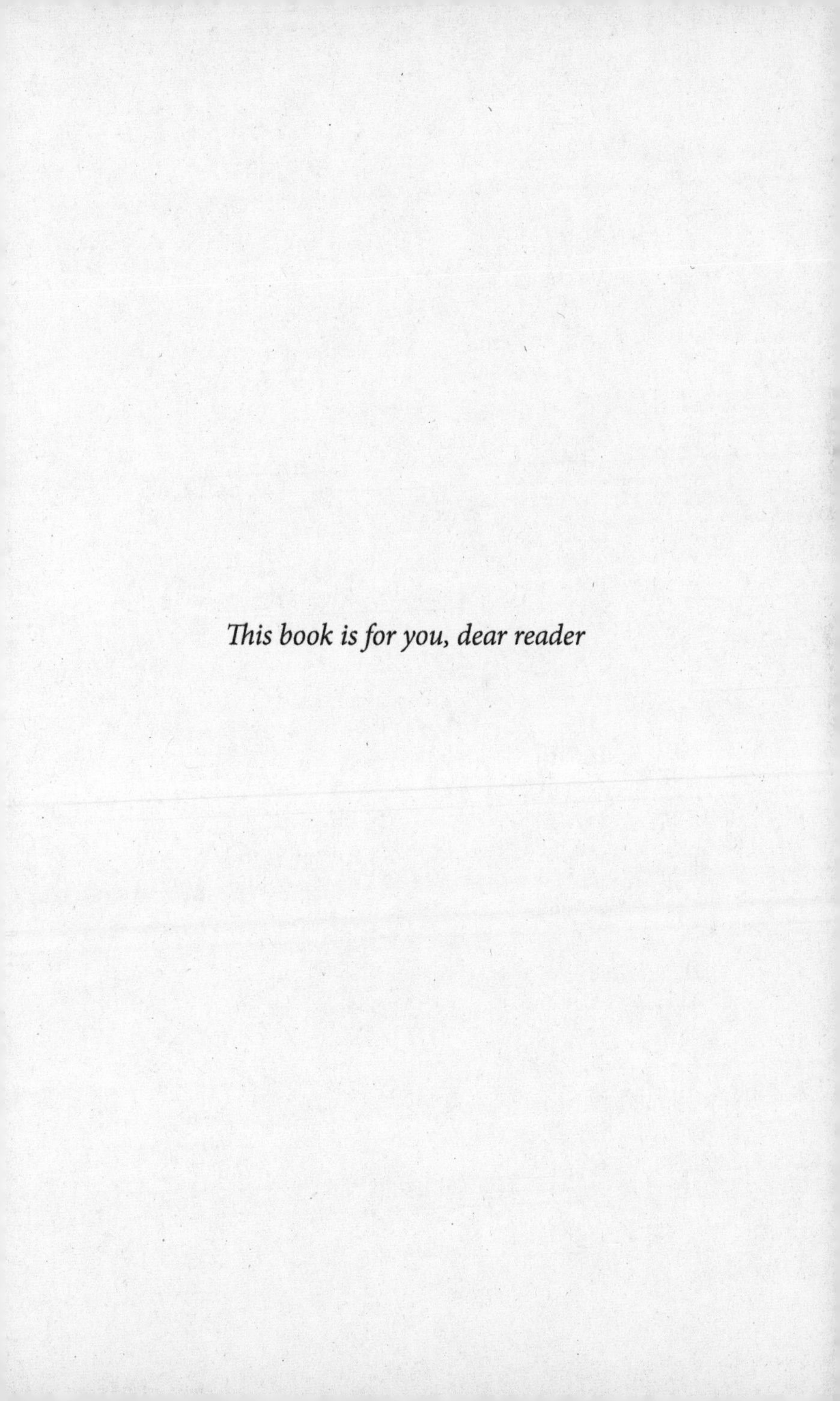

This book is for you, dear reader

CONTENTS

INSPECTOR DREADLOCK HOLMES: A CUCUMBER BESIDE LORD MONTAGU

Meet our hero – or anti-hero, as the case may be – Inspector Dreadlock Holmes: Caribbean-born, British-bred, Holmes in his mid-fifties, groomed dreadlocks under a dapper Windrush-style trilby, a sartorial salute to that post-war midsummer docking at Tilbury of the HMT *Empire Windrush*, his belated father, Archibald Holmes, having been one of those hope-eyed Caribbean arrivals.

Something about Dreadlock Holmes, you should know, dear reader, is that after a fling with a degree in Comparative Religion, he opted for the adrenaline buzz of a far more lucrative career in Criminology, a decision he had never regretted.

Now, a word about his fresh-faced, beret-headed rookie, Rudeyard Fly. The name Rudeyard can be traced back to the young man's father, who had a love for Rudyard Kipling, Rudyard being morphed into Rudeyard, which in his father's opinion had a more 'rootsy' ring to it. Rudeyard winked behind dark-framed spectacles as he declaimed one of his yarns, with thespian flair: 'Ah, to be a fly on the wall!' Hence by the Fly nickname his son was known to all.

At this moment in time, Inspector Dreadlock Holmes and rookie Rudeyard Fly are heading to a crime scene in Middleham-by-Sea – a little town known for tea shops, pet shops, florist shops, charity shops, vintage odds and ends – in short, a rustic retreat for naughty weekends. If you have any doubts as to the exactitude of the location, it's enough to say Middleham is situated, as the crow flies, halfway between south-westerly Land's End and most northerly John O'Groats.

Now, dear reader, this is off the record, but something you should also know is that the Middleham Criminal Investigation Department had deliberately requested the transfer of two black law enforcers to the quintessentially Anglo-Saxon town of Middleham-by-Sea. A way of kick-starting their diversity policy. Inspector Dreadlock Holmes and Rudeyard Fly both thought this was an opportunity too good to miss. A chance to prove their cross-cultural mettle, despite the uprooting from challenging, multi-coloured South London to monochrome Middleham-by-Sea.

And Inspector Dreadlock Holmes has already received an anonymous call, informing him that Lord Montagu, a controversial political figure, has been found unconscious beside a cucumber. Why a cucumber and not a courgette? Or, for that matter, a marrow? Such cerebral speculation would be considered a diversion from law enforcement.

'Get moving, Fly,' Holmes says, putting on his trilby.
'Why a cucumber, Chief? This guy must be veggie.'

Holmes ignores Fly. 'No time for joking, man. Go!'
Meanwhile, Holmes relishes a lungful of tobacco.

At the wheel, Fly decides to go the scenic route,
navigating the precipitous sea-fronting road

that cradles the little town of Middleham-by-Sea.
Under evening's starling sky, Middleham's elderly

can be seen enjoying the air they'd call 'bracing'
and fresh-faced couples on heat are interfacing

not just with Facebook in some airy cyberspace
but via the more direct snog-on face-on-face.

Holmes points towards the twilight-tinted cliffs,
breathing in tobacco with the sea's salty whiffs.

'Lovely view, eh, Fly? Now you see why the filthy
rich like their little cottage in Middleham-by-Sea.'

'To tell the truth, Chief, this Middleham is a little too
weird for me. Mind you, that's just my point of view.

So what's wrong with a good old-fashioned crowbar?
Only in Middleham a burglar would use a cucumber!'

Holmes smiles. 'No doubt the work of an amateur.
But that cucumber might have a lot to answer for.'

After much upping and downing, they find Poppy View,
the cottage taking its name from the yearly bloom

of poppies that register their regimental presence
along the driveway to the Montagu residence.

Holmes is about to ring the bell, when a woman
appears in bronzy sunbed tan and matching kaftan –

a woman of diva-like demeanour, to put it mildly.
Holmes imagines her stepping straight out of Puccini.

'Welcome, Inspector, do come in, I'm Lady Montagu.
May I ask the name of your colleague beside you?'

'Oh, just call him Fly. He's what's known as a rookie.
Fairly new. But Fly sure got an eye for the spooky.'

'Do you gentlemen fancy a brew of additive-free
super green tea? Unless you'd rather have coffee?'

'A cuppa would be great, thanks. In fact, spot on!'
'With organic super green tea, you can't go wrong.'

Soon Lady Montagu swirls back to the living room
with a tray of fancy blue teacups. 'Butterfly bloom

by Wedgwood,' says Lady Montagu. Holmes simply nods.
'Nothing comes close,' she adds, 'to china from Harrods.'

Something else you should know, dear reader, is that from
his small days Inspector Dreadlock Holmes had always been

prone to a condition known as Hyperactive Word Association Syndrome – abbreviated to HWAS and pronounced HWA, the S being extremely silent.

This being the case, from the moment Lady Montagu uttered the word 'china', his mind had taken flight to a Chinese takeaway of sweet and sour ribs, preceded by a steaming bowl of wonton soup. Even a passing reference to foul play, which happens regularly in his line of work, can relocate his mind back to his grandmother's sun-hot Caribbean back yard, boisterous with clucking fowls – his feathered friends, as he called them. Under the well-pleased guidance of his grandmother, small-boy Dreadlock was only too happy to perform the daily task of throwing handfuls of corn to the fowls, and come evening, chasing them back into their pens.

Freudians may be inclined to suggest that this early playful interaction with fowls could well have subconsciously prepared Dreadlock Holmes for the more sinister face of *foul play*. Thankfully, such mental peregrinations do not undermine his focus. He has tunnel vision when required.

Holmes gets out his pipe but is having second thoughts.
'Feel free to smoke,' says Lady Montagu. 'Why not?

After our Sunday morning champagne and caviar,
there's nothing we enjoy more than a Havana cigar.

Who gives a fig if such cigars are communist?
Ah, that aroma … tell me, what's there to resist?'

Fly's eyes, upwardly mobile, are busy observing
the ornate mirror perched way up on the ceiling.

Mind you, Fly thinks to himself, what an odd
location for a mirror, even one from Harrods!

But maybe there are folks who find it appealing
gazing at themselves gazing back from the ceiling.

'Ah, you're admiring our mirror. From Fornasetti's
designer collection. Just a little surprise pressie

my Lord Montagu got me for last Valentine.
My dear husband has fine taste. Very fine.'

For someone who had nearly lost her hubby,
Holmes can't help thinking she appears quite jolly.

'Any news of Lord Montagu from the hospital?'
'Oh yes, Inspector, they did give me a call.

The good news is that his condition is stable.
But why a cucumber on the bedside table?'

'Was Lord Montagu by any chance vegetarian?'
'As it happens, Lord Montagu and I are both vegan.'

'Lady Montagu, is your husband the type of chap
who'd be partial to a cucumber for a nightcap?'

'Not to my knowledge. Normally he would retire
with a whisky. Not good for his blood pressure.'

'Did you find anything missing? Say an antique?
Jewellery? Passport? Any valuables, so to speak?'

'No, Inspector, everything was in shipshape order.
Except, of course, for that mysterious cucumber.'

'We'll get to the bottom of this cucumber affair,
trust me, Lady Montagu,' Inspector Holmes declares.

'But is there anything you might not be telling us?
Lord Montagu, we know, stirred up quite a rumpus

by openly supporting the pulling down of statues
of those who'd thrived on slave-owning revenues.'

'It's true my husband had made himself enemies.
He's been called names like loony and commie!'

'Does he by chance have a Russian connection?'
asks Holmes. 'What if the cucumber was poisoned?'

'No disrespect, Inspector Holmes, but let's remember:
who'd do such a thing to an innocent cucumber?'

Then Holmes gets a Eureka moment. An epiphany!
'Lady Montagu, does your husband have an allergy?'

'Allergy, did you say? There was that one time in Geneva
when he came down with a sudden bout of hayfever.

We shrugged it away. Thought it was just a one-off.
But the other day, I saw him itch, I heard him cough.

That was after he'd scoffed half a honeydew melon.
Mind you, he'd been on the booze. A whisky marathon.

"Darling," I said, "like you've got a permanent hangover?
But I've read somewhere a good cure is cucumber".

That's the moment rookie Rudeyard Fly (who fancied
himself a bit of a gardener) mentions ragweed.

'No offence, Fly, but tell me what ragweed's got to do
with the comatose condition of Lord Montagu?'

Fly smiles. 'Well, Chief, from what I know of botany,
melon and cucumber belong to the ragweed family.'

'If so, it follows Lord Montagu must have an allergy
to melon and cucumber. Elementary, Fly, elementary.

Didn't you, Lady Montagu, say you've read somewhere
that a cucumber cures a hangover? It's pretty clear

Lord Montagu must have followed your suggestion.
His allergic reaction was a foregone conclusion.

Lady Montagu, that's all there is to this mystery.
The cucumber I won't subject to further enquiry.'

'Silly man! So sorry for all the bother, Inspector.'
With that, they say a streetwise 'Respect,' to her.

Lady Montagu then escorts Inspector Dreadlock Holmes and rookie Rudeyard Fly to the poppy-lined driveway.

'Do drop by, Inspector, when you're in the area,' she says. 'You know where we are.'

Inspector Holmes finds himself nodding.

'I'll hold you to that promise, ya?' says Lady Montagu as she sees them off, her kaftan billowing around her generous contours in the late September light of an Indian summer. If she had burst into an aria worthy of La Scala, Holmes would not have been surprised.

After minutes of saying nothing, Fly is set to tease, or as they say in the Caribbean, set to tantalise Holmes. 'Well, Chief, you gone all quiet on me. So what you think of our Lady Montagu?'

'Not what I think, Fly, what I *deduce*. In this crime work, not only your eyes but your ears have to be tuned in like a musician. Tuned in to different registers of speech. When we interrogated her inside the house, observe how Lady Montagu sounded all posh. But once she was outside on the driveway, she was more relaxed, and you heard how she slipped into "ya"?'

'So what "ya" got to do with it, Chief?'

'That Ya is a dead giveaway. When people are stressed out, or on the other hand, chilled out, they have a way of slipping into their first language. Before she married Lord Montagu she used to be an opera singer by the name of Abigail de Mendoza. Portuguese-Jewish extraction. After migrating to South Africa as a child, she had been speaking Afrikaans.'

'Amazing! How you deduce all this, Chief?'

'Simple. I took the precaution of googling Wikipedia. Apparently, her husband was a radical journalist in South Africa in the bad old days of apartheid. He got into trouble with the regime for his anti-apartheid views. Funny how the couple should end up in Middleham-by-Sea of all places. Just goes to show you, Fly, you can't judge a place by face value. Even in this sleepy little English town, you'll find one or two radical elements.'

'Never mind all that radical stuff, my question to you, Chief, is whether or not you intend checking out our Lady M? I couldn't help noticing the way you were casting an appreciative eye on the contents inside that kaftan!'

'That's where you're wrong, Fly. I was observing her elegant fingers. Her well-manicured gestures. And I bet you didn't take note of the fact that Lady Montagu had an extra little finger on her left hand?'

'But you still haven't answered my question,' Rudeyard Fly says, ignoring Holmes' last remark. 'Whether or not you plan on taking her up on her offer of "dropping by"? Not even for a cup of additive-free super green tea? Come on, Chief.'

Not being the effusive type, and accustomed to Fly's persistent probing, Inspector Dreadlock Holmes merely responds in a tone of dispassionate Received Pronunciation: 'Well, dear boy, one never knows where one may find oneself at any given time.'

INSPECTOR DREADLOCK HOLMES: A VICTIM IN FLANNEL WHITES

For those American tourists who might be clueless as to the ins and outs of glorious uncertainty, Middleham Cricket Ground is their chance to witness the game in the most idyllic of settings, with hedgerows perfect for badgers to bed in. The nearby stream, caught between oak and sycamore, has itself been known to catch the odd six or four, and the flint-walled pavilion dating back centuries gives the visitor the impression of a lush green amphitheatre for the quintessentially serene.

One day, an unknown caller (presumably no hoaxer) gets through to Chief Inspector Dreadlock Holmes.

'So, a middle aged gent in flannel whites,
did you say? Sorry, but this is a very bad line …

Yes, a middle-aged gent in flannel whites …
got that … collapsed – yes? In a heap?

For a moment I thought you'd said in a sheep?
Never mind … where? Middleham Cricket Club?'

In a flash, Inspector Dreadlock Holmes and his back-up man, rookie Rudeyard Fly, are off to the crime scene. But for the sake of clarity, dear reader, and in order to avoid any libel suit, Middleham-by-Sea Cricket Club (whose members like to think of themselves as the village green's answer to the famous MCC) is in no shape or form to be identified or confused with Marylebone Cricket Club – home to no less than Lord's, described as the Mecca of cricket and whose history dates back all the way to 1814 when Thomas Lord purchased what would turn out to be the prestigious turf at St John's Wood. And Rudeyard Fly, who is a fount of cricket trivia, seizes the chance to regale the ear of Dreadlock Holmes, who is more into a round of golf, despite Irish Socialist George Bernard Shaw's view of golf as 'a nice walk spoilt'.

So here's Fly, like a man about to burst into song:
'My old man (may he rest in the Great Beyond)

had the distinctive pleasure of being present –
eye-witness, yes – to the memorable 1950 event.'

'Ah, 1950 – the year Truman approved the H-bomb,'
Inspector Holmes retorts in a tone, somewhat glum.

'Chief, like we singing from two different hymn sheet?
No, man, I referring to the day West Indies beat

mother England in the game of glorious uncertainty.
And my old man (bless him) had proof of certainty –

a piece o' paper autographed by dem two spin twins,
you know who I mean – Valentine and Ramadhin.'

Holmes had heard that story on many an occasion,
not to mention Fly's high-pitched rendition

of Lord Beginner's calypso, 'cricket lovely cricket,
at Lord's where I saw it, cricket lovely cricket.'

But today Inspector Holmes puts Fly off his stride.
'Not now, man. We here to investigate a homicide.'

At the pavilion they're met by Captain Sideburns,
a fast bowler known for eccentric behaviour –

like starting his run-up to the crease backwards!
Pointing to the covered-up body, Captain Sideburns

sighs, 'Poor William Goddard! All padded-up at tea.
Just about to tuck into his scones with strawberry

and Devonshire clotted cream … then, my God!
Next thing you know … the fellow pops his clogs!

But you haven't heard the heart-breaking bit.
WG was 99 – *99 not out* – then misfortune hit!'

'My condolences,' Holmes says, by way of sympathy.
Rudeyard Fly is not backward in saying, 'I agree.'

'What a time for the Grim Reaper to strike you down.
Life ain't fair, *99 not out*! One run from a ton!'

Inspector Holmes steps in, puffing on his pipe,
'Tell me, Captain, can this be the work of a rival side

who might have it in for this Goddard? Or WG?'
'Inspector, are you suggesting that the SCC,

our rivals, are behind this? The SCC hate our guts.'
Captain Sideburns spells out SCC with no ifs or buts.

'Satan's Cricket Club! They just won't forgive and forget
that time, donkey's years ago, the *Middleham Gazette*

dubbed us "Local Lord's" and compared our site to heaven.
I shudder to think a member of Satan's eleven

would stoop so low as to commit a heinous crime.'
'These SCC guys might have the Devil on their side,'

Holmes reminds him, going into contemplation gear.
'Tell me, Captain Sideburns, did I actually hear

you refer to the unfortunate victim as WG?'
'I did indeed, Inspector. WG's full name, you see,

is Willow Goddard Grace – a descendant of no less
than William Gilbert Grace. Who would have guessed?

Yes, Dr W.G. Grace himself! The father of cricket!
And his now dead descendant never let us forget it.'

'Captain Sideburns, did you notice anything fishy at tea?
Anything odd while nyamming scones with strawberry?'

With a puzzled look, Captain Sideburns asks, 'Jamming
scones? You know as well as I do, scones have jam in.'

Rookie Fly laughs. 'Not jamming, Captain. Nyamming.
Nyamming means eating. A West Indian way of talking.'

'I wasn't, as you say, nyamming scones. That's the truth.
Never touch the stuff, though I admit to a sweet tooth.'

'Take time to cast your mind back, Captain Sideburns.
Did you by any chance hear WG say any last words?'

'As it happens, something he said I clearly remember.
Before he snuffed it, he said, "My shoes are on fire!"'

At this point, Inspector Holmes, in one of his verbal flights, recalls those very words being uttered by his grandmother after a day of jumping up behind the steel-band in a fit of carnival fever. 'My shoes on fire! Boy, I say, granny shoes on fire!'

But Fly, not one to miss the chance to pontificate on cricket, the game described by the late US comedian Robbie Williams as 'baseball on valium', decided to update Inspector Holmes on Dr W.G. Grace, the victim's much-revered ancestor. Various sources have led Fly to believe that the so-called father of cricket was one cheater not backward in coming forward. Once, after being clean bowled, this same Grace puts the bails back on. Yeah, man. This bare-face Dr W.G. just ignores the umpire's finger.

Then he says to the umpire, 'The folks here came to see me bat, not to see you give me out!' The doctor was also a bit of a prankster. Legend has it that on one occasion he in fact set fire to a certain fast bowler's shoes.

'Well, Fly, them burning shoes set me down the trail
of the supernatural. Now my mind in a occult frame.

I thinking karma. According to the Hindu concept,
the misdeeds of a past life follow you to the next.

Or in the words of my West Indian granny,
"What one generation sow, future pickney go reap".'

Captain Sideburns now looks in his discomfort zone.
'Must dash, Inspector. Sorry. Duty calls. Time for scone.'

'Oh no, not so fast. Just a moment, Captain Sideburns.
What's this 'bout time for scone? Pretty sure I heard

you say you don't touch the stuff. Why all the haste?'
reasons Holmes. 'So let's see what's in your briefcase.'

'By all means, Inspector. Be my guest. All you'll see,
I assure you, is nothing, nothing out of the ordinary.'

In the briefcase Holmes comes across old newspaper cuttings (pertaining to cricket), out-of-date lottery tickets, obituaries of the famous, a half-eaten banana. Nothing incriminating. Amidst this odd assortment Holmes also notices an empty medicine bottle, with a doctor's indecipherable signature. Holmes can't help thinking that back in the old colonial days in the Caribbean, those teachers who believed in double-lined exercise books as a way of enforcing the doctrine of good handwriting would surely have administered a smack on the knuckles of any doctor who had owned up to such a signature.

But why that empty medicine bottle labelled *invega sustenna*? To the best of Holmes' knowledge this was one of the drugs used for treating people of schizophrenic disposition. Holmes keeps the observation to himself and hands the briefcase back to Captain Sideburns, who is shifting from foot to foot.

And eyes straight ahead, as if staring in a stupor,
Captain Sideburns says, 'I'm descended from no other,

than Cannonball Jack, you heard me? Cannonball Jack!
Not to be confused with that Joker in the pack.

Cannonball Jack, Great-great-great-great-grandfather,
got the nickname from the way he would canter

up to the crease – then he'd let out a loud *Boom!*
Heard that, Inspector? There he goes again. *Boom!*

Do you know Cannonball Jack? He was the fast bowler
whose lucky shoes W.G. Grace had set on fire?

And my long-departed ancestor, Cannonball Jack
always dreamed of the day he'd get his own back.

Never did. The hurt went with him to his cremation.
And that hurt passed from generation to generation.

I keep hearing and seeing Cannonball Jack in my head.
"WG's the bastard who set my shoes on fire! I wish him
dead!"

Lo and behold, WG snuffed it while scoffing scones.
And Cannonball Jack must've been rolling in my bones.

It was payback time. Tit for tat. At last my ancestor
can rest in peace, move on – yes, call it closure.'

Behind spirals of smoke, Inspector Holmes nods.
'These matters, Captain, are in the hands of the gods.

We won't be proceeding with further investigation.
Meanwhile, Captain, please stay on your medication.'

'Speaking of which, Inspector, I do need to collect
my prescription. Sometime I wish I dare forget.

That's it. Done and dusted. So, Inspector Holmes,

will you be joining Cannonball Jack for some scones?'

'Not today,' Holmes replies, placing a hand on Captain Sideburns' shoulder. 'Tell you what, come with us to the station. We're not arresting you or anything like that. Just want to make sure your prescription is all sorted. Once that's done, we'll drive you home. Door to door delivery, how's that?'

Captain Sideburns is about to go in the back seat of the car when he suddenly stops and turns to Inspector Dreadlock Holmes and Rudeyard Fly.

'I'll go on one condition,' he says. 'That you take the scenic route. Heard me?'

Holmes nods. 'The scenic route it shall be.'

And Fly agrees. 'We could all do with a little sea breeze, eh Chief?'

INSPECTOR DREADLOCK HOLMES: BODY IN A LIBRARY

On a sunshine-promising October morning, Inspector Dreadlock Holmes basks in a glimmer of hope for what the Brits call an Indian summer. Rookie Fly replies, 'Chief, we can always live in hope,' keeping a keen eye on the overhead conditions like an umpire with meteorological premonitions. But right now Inspector Holmes is occupied with the more pressing matter of a possible homicide.

'Who'd want to bump off somebody in a library
in a quiet little town like Middleham-by-Sea?'

asks Inspector Holmes. 'A bookworm maybe?'
rookie Fly laughs, his black notebook out and ready.

'This is no time for joking, Fly. Murder of a literary
kind we have here. Elementary, man, elementary!'

In quick time, they're at the library, a timber-walled
converted barn that still exudes a rural charm.

'How say we question the librarian who discovered
the body this morning for possible leads?'

'Hold that thought there, Fly. Today happens to be
Thursday, so, yesterday was obviously ...'

'Wednesday by my reckoning, Chief. And the sign
outside says *Wednesday Closed All Day*.'

'Well spotted, Fly, you learning this crime work fast!
But if closed, who witnessed the victim breathe his last?

That, my boy, is clearly the million dollar question.
The time is now to interrogate that librarian.'

Having been conditioned by across-the-counter contact with the librarians of his childhood, those smartly-attired ladies who were quick to put a finger to their lips, an almost imperial gesture in honour of the God of Silence, Holmes had always linked them to a demeanour he'd call 'correct'. Nothing like the one who stands before him now, with her Gothic-midnight hairdo, the nose-ring, not to mention the dragon tattoo breathing fire from the magnolia dome of her left shoulder. The word that comes to mind is 'cool', to use the common parlance.

'Sorry about this awful business. I'm Hannah Goodwin.'

Inspector Holmes detects a certain streetwise tone.
Suddenly he is transported out of his comfort zone.

'What shall we call you? Miss Godwin?' Holmes says.
'Or Ms Godwin? One can't be too careful these days.'

'Goodwin. Not Godwin. Much of a muchness.
  Hannah will do.
But I guess you guys must be gasping for a brew?

All we've got on offer is Earl Grey, hope that's all right?'
'Splendid,' says Holmes in a tone you'd describe as polite.

'I have nothing 'gainst Earl Grey,' pipes in Rudeyard Fly.
'The name sort of blends in with the English sky!'

'How about a cupcake to keep the worms at bay?'
Fly says, 'I could murder a mug-cake, if that's okay?'

'Just ignore him, Miss Goodwin – sorry, Hannah.'
Holmes smiles. 'He has a weird sense of humour.'

To put her at ease, he launches into light conversation.
'On our way here we passed a tea shop by the station.

Mrs Beeton's is the name, I recall. I was impressed.
Any relation to Mrs Beeton, the domestic goddess

famous for her boiled egg recipe with curry powder?'
'Not to my knowledge. But you'll find, Inspector,

Mrs Beeton was no fuddy-duddy Victorian matron,
but a piano-gifted young woman. Just twenty-one.'

'Never knew that. Always thought she was an oldie.
I meant of course a citizen of the third age. Sorry.'

'No need to apologise,' Miss Goodwin says calmly.
Soon she's back with the Right Honourable Earl Grey.

Inspector Holmes says, 'Just what the doctor ordered.
Now that is what I call an excellent cuppa.'

Then Miss Goodwin's face grows suddenly sombre.
'What a shame that this should happen in October.

Library staff had been so looking forward to today:
the launching of our Black History Month display,

first of its kind to be held in Middleham-by-Sea.'
'Bad timing,' says rookie Fly by way of sympathy.

Inspector Dreadlock Holmes nods with gravitas.
'Well, what can I say, Miss Goodwin, except alas!

As the Good Book puts it, no man knoweth the hour
nor the day when cometh the Grim Reaper.

But take heart, Miss Goodwin, my man Fly and I,
are on the case. We'll probe the how till we find the why.

So any detail, however trivial, that you can pass on,
you never know, might shed light on our investigation.'

Holmes reaches for his pipe from his tweed coat.
He hesitates between to smoke or not to smoke.

But Miss Goodwin stops him in the nick of time
(or should that be in the nicotine of time?)

'Sorry, Mr Holmes, I myself do have the odd rollie,
but I am afraid that here in Middleham-by-Sea

sadly there is what's known as zero tolerance.
Smoking outside's a drag, I know. Bloody nuisance!

I got a shock,' she goes on, 'to find Mr B slumped over
the last book he must have been reading – *Staying Power*.

'*Staying Power*? How ironic!' says Inspector Holmes,
whose squinting brow shows he's in ponder mode.

'Miss Goodwin, let me examine the book in question.
It might well prove crucial for forensic inspection.'

'No probs, Inspector,' says the librarian. And only too willing to help in the investigation, she produces an old blue hardback. 'A first edition,' she explains. 'Normally it's for reference only, but we'd put it on display for our Black History Month exhibition.'

Holmes gives the book a quick thumb-through. Takes note

of the first page where someone has scribbled in the margin. Beside the sentence *Africans were in England before the English came*, there was the comment *good on you, brother*, which Holmes deciphers from the shaky scrawl. He draws this to the librarian's attention.

'Oh my God!' she exclaims. 'Some idiot, I see, has been doing some annotating! Luckily, it's in pencil.'

Holmes smiles. 'That idiot, as you put it, can only point to your Mr B, since you found him slumped over this book, which as you said is a reference copy.'

'Come to think of it, Mr B always kept a couple of pencils next to him when reading.'

'So what's so special about this book?' Holmes asks.

Miss Goodwin goes on to explain that *Staying Power* was ground-breaking. First published in 1984 by Pluto Press, it traces the Black presence in Britain all the way back to Roman times, centuries before the docking of the HMT *Empire Windrush* in 1948. The author, Peter Fryer, begins by saying that Africans were here in Britain centuries before the English came.

'I must say, Miss Goodwin, this is all very revealing.
School taught me 'bout kings, queens, beheadings.'

'Same here,' says Fly. 'Nothing 'bout black Romans in toga
arriving in England before dem invading Saxons took over.'

'Too right,' puts in Miss Goodwin. 'Nothing at all.
A black emperor, Severus, even supervised Hadrian's Wall.'

Holmes says, 'Hang on, hang on right there, Miss Goodwin.
That's a whole heap of info to take in at one sitting.

But I have a hunch, or you can call it a sixth sense,
that the old fellow could possibly have been homeless.

What better place to escape the cold and stay warm
than a library? I see no signs of grievous bodily harm.

Locked in with all these books must have felt like paradise.
Seems he died of natural causes, as far as I can surmise.'

'Poor Mr B,' says Miss Goowin. 'We all know him as
Mr B.
White Zimbabwean with a name like Theophilus Beleni

Always kept himself to himself. A regular borrower.
To us he was like part of Middleham library furniture

He'd be in the same chair scribbling away. Apparently,
the poor man was writing a book on Black history.'

'Well, well, only goes to show how we Brits complex,'
says Holmes. 'A white African researching blackness

ends up dead in an English town – Middleham-by-Sea!
Miss Goodwin, very strange, this thing called destiny.'

On the way back to base, Inspector Dreadlock Holmes takes

a deep pull on his pipe, turns to Rudeyard Fly and says, 'Elementary, Fly, elementary. My guess is that the old boy must have had a stroke.'

And the autopsy results did confirm Inspector Dreadlock Holmes' hunch that the old boy, who was homeless, had in fact suffered a fatal stroke.

'Ah, to be a fly on the wall!' sighs Rudeyard Fly, who needs no encouragement to chuck in a bit of philosophy from cricket, his other obsession apart from fighting crime. 'You see, Chief, why I keep telling you golf is just escapism, but cricket, man, cricket is life. One fatal stroke, and is gone you gone! Just so, your innings come to an end.'

Holmes smiles. 'That's the whole point, Fly. A round of golf helps me escape from thinking too much about umpire God sticking a finger in the air!'

INSPECTOR DREADLOCK HOLMES: A LITTLE SPYING

Ensconced in his lodgings, a rented oak-beamed sea-view cottage, complete with the primeval perk of an open wood fire, Inspector Dreadlock Holmes is reconciled to a night-in of solitaire chess to test his noodles, though a reader allergic to noodles may prefer the sound of solitaire chess to exercise his grey matter.

Having eventually captured enough kings and queens for an alternative royal family, Inspector Holmes decides to 'take the air' like an English gent. Nothing like a brisk walk as an overture to a sound sleep. And there he is, as we speak, walking with no destination in mind, just letting his feet take him where they will, until he passes a neighbourhood that seems familiar. That poppy-lined avenue leads, as the gods would have it, to the door of the Montagus' residence, where a shadow behind the curtains points to flesh-and-blood activity. Since Lady Montagu had said it was okay for him to drop by when he was in the area, Holmes is caught in a Hamlet-like dilemma.

To buzz or not to buzz, that is the question!

Without further dithering, he presses the buzzer; his logic surrendering to the demands of his bated breath.

'Ah, do come in, Inspector Holmes. Lovely to see you.
Shall we sit out on the patio and enjoy the view?'

'Don't get me wrong, Lady Montagu, this is a small town.
If you don't mind, shall we sit inside? Viva discretion.'

'You're dead right, Inspector. How thoughtless of me.
Imagine if someone like yourself, a pillar of society,

were caught mixing business with what's called pleasure.
So shall I do you super green tea? Or something stronger?

Fancy a glass of my own home-grown blueberry wine?
Good enough for Bacchus, good enough for mortal kind.'

'I won't say no to a drop of your home-grown blueberry.
Tonight I'm off-duty, but tomorrow I'm up early.

'So how's Lord Montagu?' Holmes asks (to break the ice).
And savouring the blueberry vino, he sighs, 'Very nice.'

'Lord Montagu is back to his old self. Chirpy and bright.
In fact he's buggered off to London. Spending the night.

Hardly around these days. Let's not discuss Lord Montagu.
I'd rather hear about you, Inspector. Tell me about you.'

'Where to start, Lady Montagu,' says Holmes, as if bemused.
'How English we've become. Haven't we been introduced?

So let's be done with all this Lady Montagu formality.
The name's Abigail. But everyone just calls me Abby.'

'I'll stick with Abigail,' says Holmes. 'It has a certain ring.
Biblical, if you know what I mean. A special something.'

'Can't say the last day anyone has called me Abigail.
I'll call you Dreadlock, shall I? I must admit I hate it,

the way Brits shorten names to Mags, Daz, Tone, Les.
Don't worry, I shan't be shortening yours to Dread.

Oh, perish the thought! I like the way Dreadlock rolls
off the tongue. Rather quaint, don't you think?' All Holmes

can respond with is something of a proverbial nature.
'They say in the dark a good name maintains its lustre.'

'Did you just make that up? You have a way with words.'
Holmes couldn't lie. 'I wish I did. No, it's an old proverb.

My grandmother was full of all these old-time sayings.
Say she's calling me and I play like I'm hard of 'earing,

she'd bawl out, "Pickney who don't hear must feel."
And back in those days parents were quick to deal

out punishment. They didn't spare the rod and spoil the child.
But without my grandma, who knows, I might have run wild.'

'Oh, she would be so proud. But detective work, I daresay,
must keep you on the go. Do you ever find time for play?'

Lady Montagu's expression is both quizzical and mischievous.
'My lips are sealed, Dreadlock, and it's just the two of us.'

'Well, as the Good Book puts it, to everything its season,'
says Holmes, smiling. 'I try to live according to reason.'

'Good Lord, Dreadlock, you're more religious than you look!
Pleasure also has its season. Never mind the Good Book.'

'In that case, I'd say golf is my green gateway to serenity.
Golf takes my thoughts away from murder, fraud, larceny,

arson, you name it. Some nights, you know, I hardly rest.
And to take my mind off crime, I turn to solitaire chess.

Can't blame you if you think this doesn't sound too exciting,
but that's how the story goes when you're law-abiding.

Of course, there is nothing like the spirit of calypso
to lift up the spirit when you're feeling kind of low.

So when my mind working overtime and I feel to chill,
I'd simply rummage through my collection of old vinyl.

Tell me something, Abigail, you ever heard of calypso?
Kitchener? Chalkdust? Short Shirt? The Mighty Sparrow?'

Lady Montagu throws back her head in abandon.
'Come on, which planet do you think I'm living on?

Have I heard of calypso? I'd have you know we had
our honeymoon around carnival time in Trinidad.'

'Apologies, Lady Montagu – Abigail – for getting it wrong.
Here's me thinking you were more into … operatic song.'

Holmes chooses not to reveal that he'd googled her and was well aware that she'd made a name for herself in the world of opera: Abigail de Mendoza, the Portuguese-Jewish soprano who, according to Wikipedia, had wowed audiences internationally. A world she seemed to have left behind. More known these days as a charming hostess who knew how to throw a party. The wife of a politician often referred to as loony and commie.

Holmes doesn't disclose any of this information, preferring to hear her past from her own lips, if and when she should think it appropriate to broach that subject. Yet the mention of opera, Holmes couldn't help noticing, had brought a fleeting cloud of nostalgia and loss to the customary sparkle of her cheeks.

'Ah, opera! Takes me back to before Lord Montagu.
To a time Abigail de Mendoza lived for rave reviews.

Though I must admit my Desdemona in Verdi's *Othello*
brought the house down. Bravo after bravo and bravo.

And as for my Donna Elvira in Mozart's *Don Giovanni*,
believe me, Dreadlock, I was an A-list celebrity.

But fame, I'm afraid, is no cure for the heart's cares.
I found out Lord Montagu was having serial affairs.

Not wanting children on my part didn't help. I dared
put motherhood on hold. What mattered was my career.

Don't know why I'm saying all this. I hardly know you.
But the other day a friend of mine spotted Lord Montagu

with an arty-farty female less than half his age. Mixed race.
It appears they were all cosy in the *café* at the Tate.

The Tate? I laughed. He'd never been keen on the Cubists.
I thought to myself he must be having a midlife crisis.

But I'll not dwell on that. Anyway, enough about me.
Shall I top you up, Dreadlock?' she asks. 'More blueberry?'

'Another glass won't hurt,' Holmes says, thinking of what
he ought to say under the circumstance. What he ought not.

To say 'so sorry to hear' he's thinking sounds rather trite.
Even to his ears, not quite right. Almost like a soundbite.

So Holmes inclines his head to hers philosophically.
'I think childhood memories can ease grown-up miseries:

I always feel better when I think back to that small boy
helping my grandmother feed the fowls. A sweet-sweet joy

would take over my soul. It's not easy to put into words,
but such thoughts give me the trust to let life take its course.'

Then Holmes pauses: 'Abigail, something you should know.
How do I put this? A little bird told me you born in Oporto.'

Lady Montagu smiles, then erupts into a girlish giggle:
'Tell me, does that little bird go by the name of google?

As for what my husband gets up to, I suspect Lord Montagu
on his last-minute London trips, is having a rendezvous

with some young miss. I thought his roving days were over.
Obviously not. I overheard him talking to some Ramona.'

'Well, if my probing, Abigail, will bring a smile to your face,
I'll keep my eyes peeled. Leave it with me. I'll be on the case.'

Holmes thinks maybe this is the moment he should leave.
Just then Lady Montagu places a hand upon his knee.

'Not always easy to seize the now. And time is so fleeting.
But the gods permitting, this won't be our last meeting.'

'Speaking of time, doesn't it fly when you're having fun?
I'll keep you in the loop about Lord Montagu's assignation.'

At the door, Holmes' heart, like her bosom, is heaving.
But he lets his logic win, though his loins are grieving.

And like a troubadour of old, his lips linger on her hand.
'You smoothie!' she twinkles. 'Well, you know where I am.'

On the stroll back to his cottage, Holmes is deep in thought. And the smoke from his pipe is not the only thing that's spiralling. Just then, a shadow appears from nowhere, almost bumping into him. Who else but rookie Rudeyard Fly?

'Jesus, Fly! You nearly made me jump!' exclaims Holmes, startled for a split second. 'I thought for a moment that someone might be spying on my movements.'

'Chief, you make it sound like dem espionage movie! No, I was looking at the twenty-twenty highlights, then I started to feel a bit itching-foot. So I just decide to step out for some sea breeze, stretch mi legs a while ...'

Between puffs of smoke, Holmes says in a calm voice, 'Well, I myself, after battling with kings and queens, thought I'd do the English thing and take the air. Very bracing ... very bracing indeed.'

'Great minds think alike, eh, Chief?'

'I wouldn't count on that, Fly. But I know you too well – you've obviously been keeping an eye on me.'

'I won't lie to you, Chief, but when I spy you out of the corner of my eye, I say to myself, Chief better mind where he walking. A man of melanin wandering round Middleham at night might provoke suspicion. So I decide to follow you in case you needed back-up – and by sheer surveillance, I see you turn in by the row of poppies leading to the residence of you-know-who. I say to myself, Ah, to be a fly on the wall. Chief, like he on night duty …'

'If you must know, Fly, since I happened to find myself in the area, I thought the spontaneous and proper thing to do would be to pop in and see how Lady Montagu had been coping. I'm pleased to say Lord Montagu has made a speedy recovery after his allergic mishap with that mysterious cucumber.'

But ever-teasing, ever probing Fly, winking behind his dark-framed spectacles, nudges Holmes. 'Spontaneous! Is that what you call it? I like it, I like it! So how's the good lady? Anything to report, Chief?'

Inspector Dreadlock Holmes merely smiles, and in the most deadpan circumspect tone he can muster, replies: 'I take it, Fly, you're referring to the weather report? Well, they say gale-force winds are to be expected.'

INSPECTOR DREADLOCK HOLMES: HOLMES GOES UNDERCOVER

Although Holmes had promised Lady Montagu that he'd keep tabs on Lord Montagu's movements in London, he must confess to having the odd moment when his conscience quivered. Not that Holmes had never done his private-eye bit. He'd penetrated insurance fraud, tax dodging, stolen identity, fly tipping, brothel harbouring. Yes, he'd done the lot. But Holmes would draw the line at spying on a wife or a husband for potential divorce proceedings. He'd rather handle an old-fashioned case of murder any day than have to snoop on marital ins and outs.

What you should know, dear reader, is that 'what God hath joined together, let no man put asunder' is a precept which Holmes does his best to apply to undercover activities. But all things considered, the Inspector decides it would cause no harm for Lady Montagu to be told what Lord Montagu gets up to on these sudden London trips.

Lady Montagu, from Holmes' observation, appears to be a woman of the world who would rather face the truth of her husband's possible infidelity than be strung along on the wings of some cuckoo fabrication. And if it turns out that Lord Montagu is not, as the saying goes, playing away from home, then what's there to lose?

So the following Friday evening finds Holmes standing on

the Hungerford Bridge overlooking the Thames. The Royal Festival Hall seems all geared up for a gig of classical music. Holmes throws a quid to a busker belting out 'My Island in the Sun' on a steelpan. Forsaking his tweed coat for an anorak and his well-polished boots for trainers, Inspector Dreadlock Holmes is undercover, observing Lord Montagu in conversation with a young lady of mixed race, possibly in her late teens. They part with a gentle peck on the cheek, more platonic than adulterous.

As the young lady, now on her own, comes towards him, Holmes plays it cool then pulls a fast one.

'Sorry to bother you,' he says, 'but the gentleman you were talking to a moment ago, I'm such an admirer, the way he supported pulling down the statues of former slave owners and all that stuff. I was hoping for an autograph…?'

'You mean my dad? Lord Montagu?' replies the young lady, her earphones plugged into her private decibels, and waltzing off with a nonchalant swagger that would not come easy to a middle-aged gentleman.

Further nosing around was about to bring forth a revelation that was the last thought on Holmes' mind. Looking back to the brief encounter on Hungerford Bridge, he does remember thinking that for a young lady, her tone of voice did sound a bit on the *basso profundo* side. Still, he admits to being surprised when he discovers that Ramona Montagu, an art student just turned nineteen, was in fact born Raymond Montagu. It didn't take long for the proverbial penny to drop. Raymond, son of Lord Montagu, was well on the way to becoming Ramona, daughter of Lord Montagu.

'Oh what a piece of work is man. (And woman!),' Holmes

says out loud, accompanied by a melodramatic sigh that Hamlet would have envied.

As for conveying his findings to Lady Montagu, keeping her in the loop, as promised, Holmes hesitates between a phone call and the personal touch. He decides on the latter, then quickly changes his mind. But after a prolonged weighing of the pros and cons, the discreet and the indiscreet, Holmes suggests they meet at Mrs Beeton's tea shop. Somewhere very English.

Somewhere neutral. Somewhere where they could have a quiet chat.

Yes, Mrs Beeton's tea shop would do nicely. Say, three o'clock, that sleepy mid-afternoon Middleham-by-Sea time of day that gives you the delusion of stepping back into 'Olde Englande'.

'Got us two seats by a window with a view of the sea,'
says already seated Lady Montagu. 'I've been naughty

and got us a couple of slices of Genoese sponge cake
topped with almond marzipan. How's that for an intake

of calories which I trust you're not counting? Oops!
So shall we be decadent and add a vanilla scoop?'

'Why not, in for a penny, in for a pound,' Holmes agrees,
though he's more genetically inclined to the spicy.

Holmes notices a sign that says *Guide Dogs Welcome*.
An old fellow in dark glasses looks very much at home.

As at home as the tea cosy around his teapot, Holmes thinks.
Part and parcel of the chinaware. Down to the blue daisy chintz.

Lady Montagu goes for a cappuccino, Holmes for a coffee.
'Is that with milk or without milk?' asks the waitress perkily,

before adding, 'These days you're never quite sure whether
some folk might take offence to the word black, whatever.'

Her say-what-comes-to-your-head directness is refreshing
to Holmes – a counterpoint to the correctness of the setting.

And after a yummy response to the topping of marzipan,
Lady Montagu gets straight down to the matter in hand.

'So, Dreadlock, out with it. What tidings do you bring me?
Did you catch Lord Montagu, shall we say, *in flagrante*?'

'Well, after a bit of undercover – as you do – ducking and diving,
the good news is there's nothing in any way compromising

between Lord Montagu and the young lady in question,'
Holmes confides. 'They share what you'd call a filial affection.'

Holmes pauses. 'Abigail … I don't know how you'll take this news

but I found out the said Ramona is the daughter of Lord
Montagu.'

He goes on: 'If I may borrow an American expression,
she's bi-racial – mixed race – you know, brown complexion.'

He was expecting her to flip or at least appear gobsmacked.
But her tone stays calm. 'Lord Montagu had a thing for black

women. Like there was this journalist, a bright young thing
from the Caribbean – don't ask me what island – under his
wing.

That's where he took her – you could say *that* again! I can't
say I myself wasn't busy touring. Then when she got pregnant

he tearfully confessed to me the child might be his doing.
"Doing indeed!" I said. "The word that comes to mind is
screwing."

To cut a long story short, to keep out-of-sight the gestation,
And in the process preserve their unsullied reputation,

they settled for relocation. Lord Montagu got her transferred
to London where she settled. And that's the last I ever heard.

Of course, all this takes me back some two decades ago.
Then I was busy being Countess Ceprano in Verdi's *Rigoletto*.'

Charmed by her balancing act of passion and restraint,
Holmes philosophises, 'Well, the rainbow follows the rain.'

Then, broaching a delicate subject as delicately as could be,
Holmes pops the question: 'Where do you stand on trans
identity?'

Lady Montagu leans back, laughing. 'Is that a trick question?'
Then she teases him. 'Don't tell me you're about to transition?'

Lady Montagu's question unruffles Holmes' coolness and releases a fountain of laughter that spills beyond the fussy doilies and neatly arranged china of Mrs Beeton's tea shop, bringing a smile to the lips of the bored-looking waitress behind the counter, not to mention a chuckle from the blind man in the opposite corner. Even his guide dog seems to have perked up a little.

'You're not from around these parts, are you, mate?' the blind man suddenly asks in the direction of Holmes.

'South London,' Holmes says without hesitation.

'No, I meant where you really from?' Without waiting for Holmes to reply, the man carries on in a jocular tone. 'I might forget a face, but I never forget an accent. Worked on an oil tanker, you see. Retired now. But been around your part of the world. Curacao, Aruba, Surinam. There they all speak Dutch. Couldn't understand a bleeding word they said. But they do some great green rum – cor, didn't I knock it back. *Rom Berde!* That's Dutch for Green Rum, and that's as far as my Dutch goes. Your accent don't sound Dutch to my ears but I've been hearing a Caribbean rhythm – you know, sort of Bob Marley …'

'You're in the right direction. Caribbean will do,' says Holmes, not wanting to commit himself, at the same time not wanting to appear unfriendly.

'I'm an East End boy, meself. Moved here nearly forty years ago. And the locals still see me as foreign. That's Middleham for you. So what brings you here? If you're looking for work, might as well tell you, there ain't none, mate.'

Lady Montagu puts a hand to her lips, presumably to stifle a giggle, then turns to the man, forgetting that he is blind. She says, 'You're looking at Inspector Dreadlock Holmes of the Middleham Criminal Investigation Department.'

'Blimey, that's a mouthful. Fancy that! A coloured bloke keeping law and order in these parts! I wouldn't have thought there'd be much crime 'bout 'ere, unless you count nicking a bit of compost! Still, Middleham ain't a bad old place. Folk are folk wherever you go. Best of luck, mate, but now I must love you and leave you.'

Then, turning to his dog, he says, 'Come on, Lucky,' adding, 'Don't know how I'd manage without Lucky. She's all the eyes I've got left. Good girl, Lucky. Time to leave these two good people to their own devices. Chop-chop …'

With that, he glances back, a small-town Tiresias, chuckling to himself.

'Did you hear that, Dreadlock? Left to our own devices,' says Lady Montagu with flamboyant emphasis on 'vices'.

She adds, 'In the words of Mae West, that immortal dame,

"Virtue has its own reward, but no box office sales!"'

Holmes, keeping the mood light, says: 'Oscar Wilde once declared,
"I don't want to go to heaven, none of my friends are there".'

'Did he now? I must remember that. Yes, heaven, I assume, won't be a bundle of laughs. Ya! Send in the doom and gloom!'

Holmes considers this his cue for gently breaking the news that Lord Montagu's son Raymond is, in fact, in the process of transitioning into Lord Montagu's daughter, Ramona. But still playing for time, Holmes by mimetic use of an index finger, attempts to draw Lady Montagu's attention to the wayward bit of cream that is at the moment trespassing on her upper lip, just below her elegant nose. In the end, Holmes takes it upon himself to dislodge the delinquent bit of cream with a precise gallantry.

Finally, the words come out. Holmes recounts his brief undercover encounter with Ramona on the Hungerford Bridge where she'd met with Lord Montagu. And without giving away any of his sources, Holmes informs Lady Montagu that his findings had led him to the discovery of the fact that the child had been brought up by her mother in London. Certain transfers of money to her mother also point to Lord Montagu secretly contributing to the child's financial needs for a number of years.

During the silence that follows this revelation, Holmes could detect a tear forming like a tiny dewdrop on the flickering fern of Lady Montagu's eyelashes.

'I've never wanted children, but he always wanted a son.
Well, now he's got a son and daughter rolled into one.

What can I say, Dreadlock? Always takes some readjusting,
when you're suddenly told one of yours is transitioning.

Still, I'm happy for him, and to tell the truth, I'm relieved
he wasn't carrying on with some woman. Do you believe

in astrology, Dreadlock? Lord Montagu's a Scorpio. Very
secretive.
I guess you must be a Libra? Even now those scales of justice

are balanced on your brow. Tell me, am I right or am I right?'
Holmes smiles, intrigued by her spot-on intuitive insight.

'You're dead right, I'm a Libra, Abigail. Man, how
did you guess?
But to be frank, I don't subscribe to all that star-sign
hit or miss.'

'Oh, the stars have a lot to answer for. And just
so you know,
I'm a Gemini. One minute high as a kite, next minute
I'm low.

I'm ruled by those twins, Castor and Pollux.
As unpredictable
as the English weather. And like mercury … very changeable.'

Holmes, out of his astrological depth, to tell from
his expression,
says, 'Abigail, you sound like you're two for the price
of one.'

After he's said it, he thinks, Hope I haven't said the
wrong thing.
Was it a blunder to relate her duality to some
bogoff offering?

Luckily, Lady Montagu seems undisturbed by his comment.
So Holmes adds, 'Of course, I intended it as
a compliment.'

'It means a lot to me. All the snooping around you've done.
One day I may even get the chance to meet this Raymond,

my stepson – sorry, Ramona, my stepdaughter. I'm sure I will.
Meanwhile, I shan't be making a mountain out of a molehill!'

Holmes strokes his chin before replying in a proverbial kind:
'Yes, my advice to you, Abigail, is just let sleeping dogs lie!'

With that, Lady Montagu gives Holmes a kiss on each cheek, then dashes off into the early autumnal dark. Having spotted her scarf over the back of the chair where she'd been seated, Holmes considers hurrying after her with the rescued accessory. But as the gods would have it, Lady Montagu has disappeared from view.

So there's Holmes standing outside Mrs Beeton's tea shop, a somewhat forlorn knight in shining armour, holding, not some slain beast's head, but a chiffon scarf of hand-painted orchids with a little hummingbird at one end. Holmes can detect a certain scent from said scarf. Very familiar. The unmistakable odour of patchouli oil.

INSPECTOR DREADLOCK HOLMES: A SCARF IN HOLMES' BRIEFCASE

With Lady Montagu's scarf carefully tucked away in his briefcase, Holmes heads back to the police station for a 6.30 p.m. briefing with Rudeyard Fly (the emphasis being on brief). A stickler for punctuality, Holmes is at his desk ten minutes early. His rookie strides in ten minutes late.

Holmes turns to Fly:

'You know it is exactly 6.40 p.m. Greenwich Mean Time?
Ten minutes late! Is this what you mean by white man time?'

'Sorry, Chief, today is Middleham Farmers' Market Day.
I thought I'd better bypass the town centre, so away

I U-turned for the long but scenic route past the sea
to circumvent any encounter with cattle or poultry.'

Holmes then points towards Fly a gently scolding biro.
'Hear me good, Fly. Allow me to keep you in the know.

As two black law enforcers in this all-white town,
we must act like role models across the spectrum.

And that applies to how we handle the ticking clocks.
Never let the locals, or our colleagues, put us in a box.'

Fly replies: 'Right, Chief, I'm reading you loud and clear.
Anyway, what's the update on the Captain Sideburns affair?'

Holmes sighs: 'Ah, the body at Middleham Cricket Ground.
Well, I've decided to draw a line under that investigation.

Captain Sideburns is in good care,' Holmes adds with a nod.
'The poor man is back on his medication, thank God.

So that should be the last we hear of Captain Sideburns
and fast bowler, Cannonball Jack, his imaginary ancestor.'

'You know what, Chief, I'll include Cannonball Jack's name
in my never-existed Cricketers Hall of Obscure Fame –

like that little-known but big-hearted Viking
run-getter.
I refer, of course, to Rognarr-Raggy-Flannels – The-Leather-
Belter.'

'Never short of a tall tale, eh Fly?' Holmes says with a smile,
as he rummages in his briefcase to produce another file.

Suddenly Fly perks up, nose twitching here, twitching there,
as if he can definitely sniff something familiar in the air.

'What's that funny smell, Chief? I recognise that smell …
the name's on the tip of mi tongue. Man, what the hell

they call it … good for masking marijuana (apparently)
the name sounds something like patch-o-ri or pitch-o-ri?'

Holmes smiles, thinking on his feet. 'Did you say Pitch-o-ri?
Cricket still on your mind? Surely you must mean patchouli?'

'That's the one, Chief. That thing quick to smell up a place.
Jesus, Chief! Like the smell coming from your briefcase?'

At this point, dear reader, Holmes, assessing the situation,
conjures up on the spot a little – shall we say … fabrication.

'Well, Fly, as I was passing between Mrs Beeton's tea shop
and Fang and Claw pet shop – you know where – I popped

into the aromatherapist just for a nose-around. Luckily
I discovered this oil that goes by the name of patchouli.

Thereupon I tried a tester of said oil … I was in no haste.
I agree it is strong. The smell still lingers on my briefcase,

but the nice aroma lady informs me it's an excellent cure
for coughs – and since there's the long winter to be endured,

I'm playing with the idea of buying a bottle of the stuff.
You must look after your body, Fly. The freeze can be tough.'

'Tell me about it, Chief. I'll take on board what you say.
In fact, I think I'll buy a bottle of patchouli today-today.'

Returned to the warmth of his cottage, Holmes leans back in his armchair and sucks on his pipe with the contentment of a puffing Buddha, recalling how he'd narrowly escaped having to explain to Fly the reason for a patchouli-scented chiffon ladies' scarf in his briefcase. The less said, the better.

Holmes then removes the scarf from his briefcase, takes a quick whiff, wraps it neatly in tissue and puts it into a padded envelope, planning to post it the next day Special Delivery to Lady Montagu. But on second thoughts, he comes to the conclusion that it would be more gallant to deliver it to Lady Montagu in person. Why not? Needless to say, at a time and place of her choosing and convenience.

After a bout of solitaire chess, Holmes, unable to focus, decides to call it a night. Soon he's fast asleep, adrift in the whirlpool of a dream, seeing himself swinging in a hammock on the moonlit veranda of a house he recognises as his grandmother's. The old house of his early childhood. The wooden house standing on stilts with the space under, known as 'the bottom-house', where he'd played marbles. The familiar picture of Jesus on the wall with the inscription in curly-curly letters: *Bless this house, dear Lord we pray.* Everything seemed in its usual place but at the same time jumbled. And there was his grandmother singing the hymn she'd sung many a night to his small-boy ears: 'Gentle Jesus meek and mild/look upon this little child,' singing not in her usual husky, almost bluesy sort of tone, but in the crystal-splitting high C of a soprano – the kind of voice he'd associate more with Lady Montagu back in the days when she was Abigail de Mendoza basking in the bravos of her adoring audiences …

Holmes, treading the tightrope between his sleeping self and his conscious self, isn't sure what to make of the dream. Was it some kind of veiled warning? Did his grandmother feel he needed protecting? Or was she, from the Great Beyond, blowing a good breeze to bless his path towards Lady Montagu's door, which is exactly where Holmes is standing at this point in time.

So there's Holmes thinking maybe he should have
phoned her
when Lady Montagu answers the door robed in a
crimson kimono.

'Apologies,' says Holmes. 'I really ought to have phoned you.
Most inappropriate, descending like this out of the blue.'

'Nonsense! If we ruled our lives by what's appropriate,
what would this world of ours be like? A very dull planet.

So what brings you here, Inspector Dreadlock Holmes?
Nothing criminal, I trust. Do make yourself at home.'

'Oh, I meant to post you this little enclosed accessory,'
Holmes says, handing her the padded envelope. 'Memory,

is a funny thing. Lapses can happen to the best of us.
You forgot your scarf at Mrs Beeton's tea shop in a rush.'

'Well, I hope my scarf didn't cause you any embarrassment.
Imagine, a detective caught red-handed with patchouli scent!

Some hippies apparently use it to mask the smell of pot.
That might not go down too well with this Middleham lot.

But now you're here, how say we have some warming Sake?
Let's have it in these cute little cups Japanese style, shall we?'

And holding a wide-mouthed red-lacquered cup to her lips,
Lady Montagu sighs, eyes closed, as she slowly sips.

Holmes, leaning back, likewise sighs and savours the drink.
Observing his every move, she asks, 'So what do you think?'

Holmes pauses, choosing his words, as he contemplates.
'Well, Abigail, I guess it's what you'd call an acquired taste.

Having said that, it does have … let's say … a certain aroma
that goes nicely with the ambience, so to speak, of your
kimono.'

Lady Montagu smiles. 'You smoothie! I picked it up in Tokyo
back in my touring days when I played Katisha in *The Mikado*.'

With that she slips on a CD. 'Can't say the last day I've heard
this music.' And the soaring voice (which she says is hers)

wings its way towards the heights of some ambrosial sphere
while from her mascara there falls the silent aria of a tear.

'Silly me, do forgive. It's been ages since I cried –
not since that awful car crash when both my parents died.'

'Sorry to hear, Abigail. My mum passed away when I was
three.
I grew up with my grandmother who meant the world to me.'

And in the silence his eyes and hers in empathy connect.
Soon they're close enough to breathe in each other's breath.

And there and then like two snails uncurling from their
shells,
their tongues succumb to the sweetest of bewitching spells.

'Is this a good idea?' Holmes asks, weighing the pros and cons
of what, dear reader, you might describe as a delicate
situation.

And then he enquires, 'When's Lord Montagu due back
home?'
And in a matter-of-fact tone, she replies: 'He's upstairs –
alone.

I daresay he can't wait for his little fantasy to come to fruition.
You see, he's been longing for the experience of a threesome.'

To say Holmes was shaken would be an understatement.
More like thunderbolt-struck. Transplanted out of his
element.

Not funny. Yet why is Lady Montagu, head thrown back,
laughing?
She turns to Holmes: 'If you believe that, you'd believe
anything.

Oh, Dreadlock, you should have seen the look on your face!
Hilarious!
Don't worry, I was only having you on. No, it's just the two
of us.'

'Nice one, Abigail.' Holmes smiles, his expression still
bemused.
'Yes, I was clueless, all right, though I'm used to sussing out
clues.'

And ascending those stairs to her bedroom (no, to her
boudoir)
Holmes feels like he's sleepwalking towards a bountiful
harbour.

Alas, dear reader, at that precise moment (one of ill-chosen
timing)
the ears of Holmes are suddenly arrested by his mobile
ringing.

'Oh, just ignore it,' says Lady Montagu, by now regally
recumbent.
'Surely, nothing at this hour of the night can be that urgent?'

To answer or not to answer, that is the question
facing Holmes,
as he deliberates between desire and an assault
of ringtones.

At last Holmes picks up a message from his rookie.
(Untypically brief.)
'Drop whatever you doing! Call me when you get this, Chief!'

Silence. Seconds later, persistent Fly is back with another call.
'Chief, it appears a body's been discovered in the village hall.'

Holmes shakes his head to the heavens: 'Lord, have mercy!
So sorry, Abigail. But duty calls – sounds like an emergency.'

Lady Montagu, tying back her undone hair, exclaims:
'Damn! Looks like the gods are against us, but you know
where I am.'

Holmes, retrieving the part of himself she had held captive,
says, 'No rest for the wicked, and that includes a detective.'

Now see our man Holmes at the wheel of his unmarked banger, bound for the village hall, his brain a whirlwind of what-ifs. What if Lady Montagu and himself had seen through their bonding to the point of crystallisation? And, caught at that liminal border between desire and duty, what if he had chosen to ignore Fly's ill-timed message?

Holmes, in whose heart the Good Book still holds a special place, recalls how Solomon and the Shulamite had made a vineyard of their yearning. As you well know, dear reader, there were no mobile phones in the days of the Ancient Israelites, but Holmes asks himself, what if some Hebrew rookie in sandals had chosen an inconvenient moment to blow some ram's horn to summon Solomon to duty, would he, Solomon, in all his wisdom, have removed himself from the beckoning altar of Sheba's lap, as he, Holmes, had removed himself from the patchouli-scented sanctuary of Lady Montagu?

And for what reason?

All because duty calls …

Brooding on such a hypothetical Scriptural scenario, Holmes arrives at Middleham village hall, home to many a jumble sale, Macramé classes, line dancing, a book club devoted to the classics, not to mention the stamping ground for those ladies aspiring to Egyptian belly-dancing.

But on this night in question, Holmes finds the fire brigade already present at the scene, battling a building engulfed in flames.

Rookie Fly approaches Holmes. 'Chief. The village hall went up like one hell of a bonfire, according to eyewitness accounts, and a body was discovered inside. Apparently the caretaker, Mr Vigilsby, was last seen alive entering the building. Sounds like the old boy himself must have gone up in flames like a reincarnated Guy Fawkes.'

Attempting to restrain Fly from waxing too lyrical, Holmes draws him to one side. 'I don't mean to harness your enthusiasm, Fly, but do try to be a bit more sensitive in your description. There's a woman behind you crying her heart out. She may well be a relative of the deceased, and at a trying time like this, she may find your reference to a reincarnated Guy Fawkes if not offensive … well, let's say, a little upsetting.'

'Sorry, Chief.'

The woman does in fact turn out to be Mrs Vigilsby, wife of the caretaker. Still in her dressing gown and blue fluffy bedroom slippers, the woman is now swaddled in a thick navy-blue blanket, courtesy of the fire brigade. But despite the traumatic circumstance, she seems able and willing to give a statement to the 'nice coloured detective' as suggested by one of the onlookers.

Holmes overhears the description of himself as 'nice coloured detective', but bearing in mind the emotionally raw nature of the situation, he decides it's wiser to put political correctness on hold. Back in South London, he'd be part of the everyday multi-coloured spectrum, but here in Anglo-Saxon Middleham, he and rookie Fly are in the eminently visible position of being a minority of two – if you were to discount the Chinese Takeaway, an oasis for an Oriental twist on battered cod with chips.

'So, you're the coloured detective bloke?' the tearful Mrs Vigilsby asks Holmes.

'Yes, I am indeed the black detective bloke,' Holmes replies, milking the monosyllabic potential of the word 'black'.

'What can I say, Officer? My husband did say one day he'd do it, but I never did give it any mind.'

'Do what, Mrs Vigilsby?'

'For donkey's years he'd been caretaker for that old village hall, and when they threatened to give him the elbow, he's never been the same since. Just sits around the house with the world on his shoulder, then one day he says to me, he says, "Thirty-seven-odd years and that's the thanks I bleeding get – but if they think they'll be rid of me that easy they've got another think coming. I cared for that old village hall like it was bleeding family, but tell you what, luv, I'd rather burn it down meself – flipping burn the lot down, if that's what it takes. Ungrateful bastards!" But Officer, I swear he never meant a word of what he said – not a word ...'

Then from the crowd steps a young man in baggy skull-and-crossbones T-shirt, probably in his mid-twenties, but looking the worse for wear, bleary-eyed and obviously out of it.

'Shame 'bout old Vigilsby ... good as gold he was. Couldn't believe me eyes when I spotted the old village hall on fire. I thought, Flip me, what if the old boy is in there pottering around as usual. I had a mind to go in and all, but then I thought, I'll dial 999 – leave it to the fire brigade, the professionals – but they took their bleeding time getting here. There you go.'

Holmes takes a mental imprint of the individual's physiognomy, but says nothing to him, just turns to Mrs Vigilsby.

'One question, Mrs Vigilsby, was your husband a drinker?'

'You mean like an alcoholic? Good Lord, no! He never touched a drop – not a drop, Officer, not since the doctor warned him he'd be digging his own grave.'

'That will be all, thank you, Mrs Vigilsby. I'll leave you in the capable hands of Mr Rudeyard Fly who'll accompany you to the car where you can sit in the warmth and catch your breath. Then we'll escort you to the station where you can have a nice cup of tea and whatever professional help you'll be needing. I won't be a moment.'

While Fly guides the woman to the car, Holmes sees to it that all access to the village hall has been sealed off, then he decides to have a nose around the premises, for detectives are known for nosing around. Yet, strangely enough, nosiness is a quality often frowned upon by many Brits.

But whoever it was that called the nose an eye that can see objects, might have been on to something, for Holmes' nose has just led him to something shiny there between the rubble. A couple of needles.

In case, dear reader, you're thinking of your grandma's knitting needles, think again. By now of course Holmes' brain cells are in a state of overdrive. Since Mr Vigilsby never touched alcohol (according to his wife) what's a pile of Stella Artois cans doing lying there beside dodgy needles?

It doesn't need an ounce of rocket science to put two and two together, Holmes thinks to himself, as they return to the station. In the interview room, Fly nods at Holmes, and Holmes nods at Fly, who turns up the heater to banish the edge off the chill.

Then Holmes touches the distraught Mrs Vigilsby on the shoulder. 'A cup of tea, Mrs Vigilsby?'

'If it's no trouble, Officer.'

'No trouble at all.'

'Leave it to me, Chief,' says Fly, springing promptly into tea-making mode.

Holmes sits in silence observing the caretaker's wife. The aquiline nose set between pallid high cheekbones, the Wedgwood-blue eyes peering from behind a pair of round copper-framed glasses combined to give her a vulnerable birdlike appearance, as if the Creator had set out to fashion an owl, but at the very last minute had had second thoughts.

In a calm voice, Holmes says to her: 'Someone from TAP will be with you shortly.' Now, the curious reader may be wondering what TAP is all about? Well, it's one of those things you either know or don't know. But just so you do know, dear reader, TAP in fact represents the Trauma Alert Personnel who provide emotional support and counselling where needed.

But unaware of this, Mrs Vigilsby goes on: 'Did you just say tap? Why, had there been a leak? Oh dear! If it isn't one problem, it's another. After the terrible news I was at my wits' end and must have rushed out of the house and left the tap running. Before long I'll be up to me knees in water. Did you say someone will be here shortly to fix the old tap?'

Holmes and Fly both manage a smile, despite the gravity of the situation. And Holmes reassures her: 'Nothing's wrong with your plumbing, Mrs Vigilsby, and if it's of any comfort to you, I'm pretty sure your husband wasn't behind this dreadful business.'

'Oh, my Alf wouldn't dream of doing a thing like that. No, his heart and soul have always been in that village hall. He was always fixing this, fixing that, a lick o' paint here, a lick o' paint there – and much good it did him! Now it's all gone, all gone like he has and we all will. Sure thing, 'cos in the end it's just down to mortar and bricks, ain't it? Mortar and bricks, that's what.'

Holmes next instructs Fly to remain with Mrs Vigilsby until the TAP person turns up, while he steps outside for a breath of fresh air, which is Holmes' way of saying he's going out for a smoke.

So, dear reader, on the police parkway of crazy paving stone,
there's Holmes puffing his pipe as he contemplates alone.

Soon he's joined by Fly who updates him on Mrs Vigilsby.
'Chief, she's as we speak, in a heart-to-heart with the TAP lady.'

Then, to Holmes' surprise, Fly is rolling himself a roll-up.
'Something the matter, Fly? Thought you had given it up?'

Fly aaahs in and aaahs out, watching smoke rings collide.
'Chief, I find this peaceful town a little on the stressful side.

And that's the God's truth. Don't know 'bout you, but this town testing
me to the limit. It don't worry you? All the law-breakers we arresting

bound to be white. Let's face it. Middleham is after all all-white.
And that's the problem, Chief. I don't feel – you know, quite right.

In South London we'd be arresting all types – Caucasian …
Yeah man, we'd be busy nicking black, not-so-black, Asian …

Still, Chief, as black law enforcers, that kind of puts us on the spot.
Once the novelty of us is over, we might upset the Middleham lot!

No doubt the black brethren will call us all sorts of names,
like Babylon, Traitor, Coconut – but I nicking them all the same.

Be you a bigwig, be you a Joe Bloggs, whatever pigmentation,
I keeping the way open to across-the-spectrum incarceration.

Yeah man, regardless of creed, race, age, gender proclivity,
I'll be sticking to the rule of law for the sake of diversity.'

Holmes smiles. 'Well, Fly, I see you and conscience-a-wrestle.
But let me tell you, there's more to the mortar than the pestle,

as my old grandmother used to say. So take note, my boy Fly.
Check for the facts behind the facts. What don't meet the eye.

Listen me good. Read the hidden story between the lines.
Beware of double-speak spin-doctors who give sixes for nines.

The thing is always to consider the psychological
aftermath.
According to the Good Book, a gentle word turneth away
wrath.

Some white people, especially liberals, can get high on talk of
race.
But it's elementary, Fly (to keep in mind), there's a time and a
place.'

'Good advice, Chief, I certainly intend to take it well on
board.
Trust me, Chief, I'll impose the rule of law with utmost self-
control.'

Holmes nods as he puffs away. 'Well spoken, Fly, I'm
impressed.
Your future with the Police Force holds forth a bundle of
promise.

But while I do appreciate your flights of quirky oration,
I suggest you be ambivalent on the subject of incarceration.'

At the mention of incarceration, Fly's mood goes a bit broody.
'This policework ain't really for me. I plan on writing poetry.'

'Tell me why I'm not the least bit surprised,' says Holmes.
I always knew you, Fly, possessed deep down a Bardic bone.'

'That means a lot, Chief. How say I read you a poem of mine?
It's only seventeen syllables, and that's counting every line.

I thought I'd try my hand with what the Japanese call a haiku.
It's short, so it won't take long. Before you blink, I'll be through:

Under the grey of Hope and Glory
lies a hidden rainbow story.'

Holmes puffs away, listening keenly, as Fly declaims, as opposed to reads.
'That's it, Chief,' says Fly, to which Holmes replies: 'Very concise, indeed.'

Holmes, smiling, says, 'I look forward to your first published slim volume.
The flyleaf could say *By P.C. Poet Fly*. The sales might even go boom.'

'Brilliant idea, Chief. That could be like my sort of pseudonym. *P.C. Poet.*
The more I think about it, Chief, the more I like it, yeah man, I like it.'

And since a cuddle from a dad is something Holmes had missed out on,
Holmes without thinking gives Fly a bear hug like a prodigal son.

'Don't judge this town by face value, Fly. When you least
expect,
this provincial all-white Middleham might reveal hidden
depths.'

Now, Holmes may not be the first to admit it. You know what Holmes is like, dear reader. Very cagey. But can those hidden depths he speaks of perchance bear any relation, subliminally speaking, of course, to the mercurial Lady Montagu?

Holmes brushes aside the thought under an inner carpet of fantasies unfulfilled. It's been a long night. He's content to cruise in his old banger along the seafront, bask in Middleham's unpolluted night, inhale a tincture of sea air, do a detour through the cobbled byways of the old town, past the Knackers Inn that functions to this day as a pub-cum-B&B.

According to the tourist guide, the Knackers Inn goes back to the mid-eighteenth century and owes its name to the fact that the inn had been built on the site of a former knackers yard, where old farm animals and horses would be put out to endure their final hours on earth. The place where horses, no longer fit for work after a lifetime pulling overloaded wagons, would be fated to pass on to their Maker with the dubious consolation – not unlike today's organ donations – of having their manes recycled for mattress stuffing, their skin tanned for sensible shoes, their bones ground down for compost.

However, the truth according to legend, dear reader, is that the original landlord had this remarkable knack of pulling pints of Guinness blindfolded without spilling a single drop. And that's not all. Still blindfolded, he would deftly execute a Picasso-like shamrock in the creamy head of the dark brew. And in case there were any weary travellers and stragglers among the punters, while ringing a bell to signal last orders, he'd bellow like a town crier: 'Any o' you lot too knackered to leg it? Well, I've got warm rooms upstairs, where there's no fear o' getting robbed! And I'll do you a fair price. Can't say fairer than that!'

As a result, the villagers referred to him as Mr Knackered, and with time and word of mouth, the pub would evolve into the Knackers Inn.

Needless to say, Holmes prefers to trust the legend and take the guidebook with a pinch of salt and a pound of sugar, as they say in the Caribbean.

Holmes thinks to himself, Maybe this little town of quaint cottages with bay windows beckoning Georgian elegance, this little town with the crumbling (but still standing) folly of a castle, this little town whose very stones are still vestige of what used to be called 'Merrie England' … maybe this is exactly the sort of town where two black law enforcers like himself and Fly can make the world of difference – be black role models with a bit of role-play thrown in, build bridges across an abyss of assumptions. Dare to fly the tribal lock.

Holmes is amused to hear himself utter 'fly the tribal lock'. Not bad, as far as metaphors go. Maybe P.C. Poet Fly will one day come up with a haiku about flying the tribal lock!

Holmes tells himself that if poetry is built on the soil of
 paradoxes,
well, then, where better to start than by de-ticking ethnic
 boxes?

Over Victoria sponge, digestive biscuits and
assorted teas,
Holmes thinks it's okay to invoke multiple uninvited
identities.

Still awake, he turns to flicking through a golfing
magazine,
hoping green thoughts will lull his restless limbs into the
serene.

Then he stumbles on something. 'Golf,' writes some pundit or
other,
'comes from the Dutch word *kolf*, meaning club.' Well, I
never …

Known for Van Gogh, Gouda cheese, coffee shop courtesies,
I see the Dutch have put their putt and tee in English
dictionaries.

As his grandmother would say, 'The more you live, the more
you learn.'
Though he'd rephrase that: 'The more you long, the more you
burn.'

Sleep is still hard to come by, and something tells him to
check
his voicemail, as you do. You never know. And there's always
texts.

Fingers crossed, there might even be one from you-know-who.
Ah, to hear that discreet sotto voce of – you guessed, Lady Montagu.

And as Lady Luck (or should that be the gods?) would have it, there
is indeed a message. Yes, her whispered tones now cleave the air.

'Abigail here. Sorry to be a bother, but I'm in a bit of a quandary.
Lord Montagu's son (my stepson) has gone off being non-binary.

Would you believe it? He's going back to his former binary self.
No longer Ramona but back to Raymond, at least that's my guess.

But the reason I'm calling, did you in haste happen to leave behind
a maroon woolly scarf with a sort of – you know, golf clubby design?

Surely, it must be yours, from that occasion duty called you away.
Collect it in your own time – you know where I am. Have a nice day.'

Holmes promises himself he won't breathe a word to his
rookie, Fly.
and replaying her message lifteth up his spirit unto the Most
High.

INSPECTOR DREADLOCK HOLMES: LADY MONTAGU TOPPLES VERDI

Holmes wakes next morning wondering whether Lady Montagu, having re-assessed their moment of foreplay, so rudely interrupted by that emergency call to the village hall, yes, Holmes is wondering whether or not Lady Montagu would conclude that maybe it had all been for the best. Such amorous dalliance would set the tongues of Middleham wagging, if word got around.

Holmes thinks that going to her house to collect his scarf might be tempting fate. No, it would be better to meet somewhere neutral. Somewhere safe. Of course, there's always Mrs Beeton's tea shop. And in a brief phone call, that's exactly where Holmes proposes they meet, adding that since she'd forgotten her own scarf at Mrs Beeton's, it seemed almost poetically fitting for him to retrieve his scarf at the same tea shop. That sounded like a plan. That is, until he heard an unexpected message from Lady Montagu on his voicemail.

'Lord Montagu is off to the Bahamas. Taking time-out on a yacht.
He'd take me on the trip, but I get seasick. I said I'd rather not.

Besides, I've got some news, Dreadlock, I'd like to share with

you.
In private. I certainly wasn't thinking of a tea shop for a rendezvous.

I need some advice, so do pop by. Well, see how you're feeling.
Unless, of course, you find Mrs Beeton's scones more appealing …'

'Such a devil!' Holmes smiles to himself every time he repeated
that message which, dear reader, he has since diligently deleted.

Now our man Holmes rings her doorbell, no longer deliberating.
His habitual logic, in a manner of speaking, now relocating

to some tropical place that's full of mostly sweet noises
when sunset prepares its red carpet for parakeet choruses.

It's not often that Holmes is given to nostalgic imaginings,
but now his mind is back to small-boy sun-hot beginnings.

Lady Montagu answers the door, not in a kaftan or a kimono,
but this time in a jogging suit, her cheeks sweating. All aglow.

Hands akimbo, running on the spot, as hyped-up as can be,
she pours herself an apple juice and Holmes a stiff whisky.

From a silver chain, a stopwatch dangles between her bosom.
making Holmes think of some athlete blooming on a podium.

'So what's your news, Abigail? Tell me, man, I'm dying to hear.
Nothing alarming, I hope. Nothing untoward. Come on, clear the air.'

Lady Montagu smiles. 'MADS out of the blue has offered me the role
in the opera *Aida*. After all these years, I'll be treading the boards.'

Holmes can feel in Lady Montagu's voice an undeniable buzz,
but he's weighing up all the info, as a good detective does.

'One step at a time, Abigail. First of all, congrats on your good news.
But who or what is this MADS? You got me sort of confused.'

'MADS stands for the Middleham Amateur Dramatic Society,
I thought you knew? Well, they're planning to do *Aida* by Verdi.

Very ambitious of them, I must say. But the producer of the show
(a friend of Lord Montagu) knows I'm at home in the Italian lingo,

and feels confident that if I were happy to lose a little weight, then to the part of Aida I'd lend a certain weight

as well as gravitas. I must say I was extremely flattered
to hear him say yours truly will give the slave girl, Aida, some stature,

as well as presence, those good old-fashioned thespian qualities
required to match the operatic grandeur of Signor Verdi.

Mind you, I'm no spring chicken, but I'm to be an Ethiopian princess,
hence the jogging suit – must get back to a state of super fitness.'

'Once a diva always a diva,' Holmes ventures to say. 'You'll be a hit.
Grab the opportunity with both hands, Abigail. Yeah man, go for it.'

Then, raising a glass, Holmes says: 'Tell me, why I get the impression
that somewhere along the line you have a niggling reservation?'

'I'm excited, except for one thing. They'd like me to darken my face.
Aida, you see, was Ethiopian. One of the royal Nubian race.

I know Olivier blacked-up when he pranced around as

Othello,
though I'm not too comfortable blacking-up for Aida, oh no.

The director says Aida was a slave girl, so he sees nothing wrong
with a bit of blacking-up to give her, as he puts it, "a truthful complexion".

Aida, by the way, is in love with this captain of the Egyptian army.
But so is Amneris, the Pharaoh's daughter. Of course, their rivalry

has tragic consequences. In the end, Aida is condemned to death.
(Surprise surprise.) But she and her lover have this beautiful duet.

I won't bore you with details, but I'm curious to know your view,
as a Black person? What's your take on this blacking-up issue?'

Holmes pauses: 'Let me put it this way. Even with white face paint,'
he says, winking, 'I don't think I can ever pass for Henry the Eight.

And with all the beheading he did, I'd have to arrest that

Tudor.
Legally speaking, the man guilty of multiple first-degree murder.

But fun and joke aside, Abigail, opera is not exactly my forte,
so I'm afraid you will have to fill in the gaps along the way.

From what I gather, this Ethiopian slave girl, Aida, speaks Italian?
Right? So far, so good. Yeah. Courtesy of Mussolini's invasion.

But no need at all to paint your face black. With your inner fire

you can transform this slave girl, Aida, to one feisty Boadicea –
that Celtic warrior woman who kicked Roman ass in ole Britannia,

as Ashanti Nanny kicked British ass when JA was shackled to Empire.

Excuse me, Abigail, for dwelling on this business of kicking ass.
What I mean to say is, you were born to give this Aida gravitas.

Be Aida with attitude. You just be yourself with righteous
rage.
And mark my words, Abigail, you go set that stage ablaze.'

'What can I say, Dreadlock? Your words have inspired me.
And no audition required. I'll say yes. Here I come, Verdi!'

With that, she whips off her jogging top with one deft gesture.
'Good Lord, Dreadlock, I'm sweating! So humid, this
weather ...'

In the temple of his head, temptation's bells are ringing,
though a one-off one-night fling isn't what Holmes is
thinking.

But viewing at close range her unabashed pair of cupolas,
Holmes feels like he's in the middle of an Oriental drama.

Funny that Holmes' thoughts should stray towards the Orient, especially since he is still to read the Palestinian writer, Edward Said, who is on Holmes' bedside to-read list. But if you, dear informed reader, have read Edward Said, you'd know that he spells out what lay between the cultural lines of East and West, and cites *Aida* as an example of the Western world orientalising Egypt as – in his own words: 'an essentially exotic, distant and antique place in which Europeans can mount certain shows of force.'

Said goes on to say that little, if any, allowance was made for the non-European, except within the framework of Europe's expansionist imperial domain. Said argues that even the monumental opulence of Verdi's opera cannot be removed from the nitty-gritty historical context of 'the struggle for territory and control'.

Meanwhile, Holmes remains as pensive as Rodin's *Thinker*.
But being only human, his eyes are by no means blinkered.

And noticing, as if for the very first time, her extra little digit
(that God-given sixth finger) Holmes on impulse kisses it.

'Don't worry, Abigail, you know you're one well-blessed lady?
My grandmother would say extra finger means you born
lucky.'

'I guess I'll need all the luck in the world, if I'm to get away
with being a nubile Ethiopian.' Holmes smiles. 'Man, seize the
day …'

Then, Lady Montagu, slipping into a bosom-hugging T-shirt,
says, 'Dreadlock, I'm oh-so sorry to be a bit of a spoilsport,

it's just that the director meets with the cast in fifteen minutes,
so I must love you and leave you. Must dash or I'll never
make it.

As a detective, you know as well as I do, that punctuality
distinguishes professionalism from amateurish mediocrity.'

'So how does Lord Montagu feel about this *Aida* business?'
Holmes asks. 'Does he approve of your return to showbiz?'

'Well, hubby thinks I'm like Muhammad Ali returning to the ring –
the fading butterfly of a man who's past the prime of his sting.

If truth be told, he's sceptical as well as worried on my behalf.
He says if I go flat on the high notes, the town will have a laugh.'

The following morning, back at base, Fly draws Holmes' attention to the *Middleham Gazette* headline: LADY MONTAGU SET TO MAKE COMEBACK. Beside the headline a photo shows Lady Montagu in her soprano prime when, as Abigail de Mendoza, her celebrity appeal would have opera fans trepidating at the sight of her gloved hand waving through a limousine window.

'Chief, thought the article might be of interest,' says winking Fly.
'They've praised her coloratur-ass (whatever that means) to the sky!'

'Not coloratur-ass, Fly. You'll find the word is in fact colorature*a*,'
Holmes corrects him, adding, 'Like Sake, an acquired taste is opera.'

For unknown to Fly, Holmes had googled opera (as you do)
so as to keep his talk attuned to that of Lady Montagu,

even stopping off at the second-hand music shop as he passed.
He'd picked up an old vinyl by some lady by the name of Maria Callas –

a Greek-born diva, known for a tempestuous heart-aching affair,
and whose voice embodied an uplifting yet subliminally tragic air.

Unable to speak Italian (not counting espresso, pizza, spaghetti)
Holmes can now name-drop the likes of Puccini, Donizetti,

Bellini – Verdi, of course – all of that illustrious composing posse.
Thank God for the English lyrics displayed on the vinyl sleeve.

Fly says, 'So, Chief, will you be in the front row cheering her on?
Or standing in the back row giving her a "standing" ovation?'

Holmes frowns. 'You never ever let it rest, do you now, Fly?
The lady's married. Besides, if you must know, she ain't my type.'

The scrupulous would say Holmes has just told a little white
lie,
Holmes would rather say 'a little non-black lie' (if you don't
mind).

Reading through the article, Holmes scratches chin and head,
when he discovers the director is related to the infamously
dead

impresario with the inauspicious name, Alberto Antonio
Fiasco,
who had been in the public eye around the mid-1800s
or so.

There are linguists who insist the word 'fiasco' is derived
from the Medieval Latin *fiasco* (a flask for storing wine),

but according to one school of thought referred to as loony,
English owes a debt to Signor Fiasco, the showbiz personality

whose productions were doomed to predictable mishaps:
his name eponymously evolved into a synonym for
cock-ups.

Once, overhead lights suddenly fallen from the rafter
almost decapitated the soprano in mid-tragic rapture.

Apparently, the anticipation of disastrous consequences
put bums on seats. Signor Fiasco pulled in audiences.

But what now gives Holmes growing reason for concern
is when, on further perusing, he suddenly comes to learn

that the MADS director of *Aida*, one Mr Gladstone Fiasco,
is a direct descendant of the ill-luck-prone Alberto Fiasco

who, according to that digital sage, the Google Master,
had succeeded in accruing disaster followed by disaster.

An immigré to Middleham and author of a memoir (bless him)
entitled *The Show Must Go On, Come What Mayhem*.

Well, the opening night at last arrived to rave previews.
Inspector Dreadlock Holmes and Fly (not overly enthused)

mingle with Lady Montagu's specially invited A-list guests,
all set to peer through binoculars and lorgnettes.

Needless to say, Fly chooses to go down the lorgnette route.
Pleased with his choice, he's thinking, Don't I look cute?

Then Fly whispers, 'Hope it's truly over when the fat lady sings ...'
Holmes says, 'Please, Fly, talking during opera? *Not* the done thing.'

Holmes, of course, had taken his precautionary nose-around
(Fiasco still on his mind) to ensure everything safe and
sound.

The technician assured him the overhead lights were well
hung.
'Ooops! Sorry, must get this show on the road,' says the young

chop-chop female answering to the name of stage manager.
'Nothing to worry about, Inspector Holmes, nothing
whatsoever.'

So there sit Middleham's crème de la crème dressed to the
nines.
In their midst, the two black law enforcers in their tuxedo
prime.

Spot on time, the curtains open onto a panoramic backcloth
of a brightly painted baboon-featured Egyptian god, Thoth,

overlooking what looks like a barge floating towards infinity.
One little boy giggles: 'Mummy, that man looks like a
monkey!'

The mother hushes him up, embarrassed to say the least.
'That's not a man. That's a god though he resembles a beast.'

While the orchestra invokes a world of pyramids and Pharaohs,
the audience erupts into appreciative *ooohs*, *ahhhs*, *ohhhs*.

And there centre-stage, striking a pose, tragic yet most demure,
Lady Montagu belts out octaves for philistine and connoisseur.

Then comes that long-awaited final duet, the doomed lovers set
to stir every heart in the house and turn even restrained eyes wet.

Now, dear reader, if you are a fanatical follower of opera, most likely
you will know by heart some of the lyrics, even in the original Italian:

O terra, addio; addio, valle di pianti,
sogno di gaudio che in dolor svani.
A noi si schiude il ciel e l'alme erranti
volano al raggio dell'interno di ...

But for the benefit of the monolingual English speaker, here's a rough translation:

Farewell earth, farewell valley of tears ...
dream of joy that disappeared in sorrow.
Heaven closes on us and the errant souls
fly to the ray of the Eternal ...

This is the moment when the ill-starred lovers, Aida and her military hunk, Radamès, entombed under a temple, are about to take lamentation to new heights, or maybe that should be to new depths, when something quite out of the ordinary transpires, throwing the orchestra, the cast, indeed the entire theatre, into a state of unprepared-for commotion.

And the person responsible for the disruption is none other than Lady Montagu, who has taken the liberty of updating – some would say more like tampering with – the libretto. Or to put it bluntly, more like mucking up the lyrics.

Dear reader, had you been there to witness that unforgettable spectacle, which has lingered on in the cultural DNA of Middleham to this day, here follows the version you'd have heard Lady Montagu render as the ill-fated Aida.

'Farewell earth, farewell valley of tears.
Farewell, dream of joy and heaven's blue.
Shame on you, who thrived on blood of slaves.
Good riddance to your toppled statue ...'

The silence that followed was disconcertingly electric. You could have heard, not just the proverbial pin drop, but a needle falling to the ground would equally have impacted on a keen eardrum. The tension was so intense, the smallest penknife, or indeed a blunt razor blade, would have served to cut it like a slice of Victorian sponge.

But, dear reader, you haven't heard the half of it.

'Bravo! Bravo! Bravo! Well done, my darling! Good on you!' cries someone in the back row – a well-tanned Lord Montagu.

Just back from the Bahamas, he'd made it in time for the final
act where he'd witness his wife embrace the controversial.

Again Lord Montagu, known far and wide for his radical
views,
cries: 'Bravo, sweetheart! Toppling statues is bloody long
overdue.'

His denim-clad son, no longer Ramona, now back to
Raymond,
wolf-whistles and shouts out his support. 'Nice one, Mum,
nice one!'

Beside him, his black biological mum, an investigative
journalist,
gives the Black Power salute in the manner of Angela Davis.

It appears she and Lady Montagu had come to a compromise,
and for the sake of Raymond to act as adults who were
civilised.

From the audience come exclamations such as, 'Commie lot!'
Yet, hold strain, dear reader, there's more thickening to the
plot.

The lights go out, throwing every soul to the darkest of
depths.
A chandelier crashes to how many pieces is anyone's guess.

Holmes, in an instant, rushes like Sir Lancelot to the rescue.
Feeling his way to the stage, he guides Lady Montagu

by that very hand which a moment ago she'd dared to raise
in a sensational outburst of unscripted apocalyptic rage.

Luckily, Lady Montagu is unharmed, though a little shocked.
And she sighs: 'Ah, Inspector Holmes, you're indeed my rock!'

And in the darkness Holmes caresses her little extra finger,
that intriguing – shall we say – flesh and blood enigma.

All that remains to be said, dear reader, is that in the aftermath of that unprecedented state of affairs, Lord Montagu expresses profuse gratitude to Inspector Dreadlock Holmes for his heroic rescue of Lady Montagu from possible brain damage due to a collapsed chandelier – which no doubt would have tickled the grave-deep funny bone of the disaster-prone Alberto Antonio Fiasco.

'What a night,' sighs Captain Sideburns, dressed in his snazzy MCC blazer but now sadly in a wheelchair. 'What a night!' he repeats. 'Bet Cannonball Jack would have loved every moment …'

'Lady Montagu, she nailed it!' says Hannah Goodwin, the Gothic librarian, now resplendent in black off-the-shoulder evening gown, her shoulder still ablaze with that dragon tattoo, though she looks slightly out of her comfort zone with her stockinged toes protruding from precarious stilettos.

And the blind man, whom Holmes had met briefly at Mrs

Beeton's tea shop, his dog Lucky still at his side, doffs his hat and says out loud for all to hear: 'Political correctness gone bonkers, am I right or am I right, Inspector?'

And not to be outdone, in the midst of all the hoo-ha, rookie Rudeyard Fly rushes to cover with his jacket the shivering shoulders of the minimalist actress, apparently of Eastern European origin, who'd played the Egyptian princess.

'Sorry, I haven't got a technicolour dream coat. This jacket will have to do,' says Fly with a straight face.

'So awful sweet of you,' she says, giving a smile as warming as a heatwave in grey January.

'The pleasure is all mine,' Fly replies, doing his best to blush.

And the following day's papers all have their own spin. One tabloid, known for its sleaziness, carried the front-page headline: LADY MONTAGU TOPPLES VERDI.

But most endearing to the eyes of Holmes and Fly was the headline big and bold in the *Middleham Gazette*:

BLACK LAWMEN TO THE RESCUE

STOWAWAY SPIDER

With four of my spider eyes peeled on the horizon, and my other four eyes watching land disappear in the distance, I had the feeling that even the palm trees were waving us goodbye and wishing good luck to all who had placed their faith in a ship.

But in case you're wondering, well, I'm not your typical spider, but yours truly Anansi.

Ever shape-shifting grandma, grandpa, aunty, uncle, all rolled into one. And embracing now-time and long-long-ago time, I dwell on the threshold between worlds. The spider gender-bender with the insider-outsider spin on the human state of affairs.

Now, let me tell you-all something you won't find in any history book. Do you know that I, Anansi, was the undiscovered stowaway on that famous ship, the HMT *Empire Windrush*? Well, it was my old friends, the Tradewinds (who always keep me in the global loop) – yes, it was them who gave me the tip-off that the *Empire Windrush* was soon to leave the island of Jamaica. According to rumour, nearly five hundred West Indians, mostly Jamaican, would be boarding the ship bound for England.

The flying fish over blue Barbados waters, the hummingbirds reversing flight among the hibiscus flowers of Trinidad, the crabs writing their signature on the Atlantic coast of Guyana, they hadn't a clue about this breaking news.

But with my spidergram network, I, Anansi, was well into the know. I must admit when I first heard mention of ship, I was a bit worried, since a long time back I had made a journey by ship. That was the first time I'd ever seen a ship and it looked to me like a big house floating on water. But after that terrible journey, the raging sea – and don't talk about the rocking, the tossing, the clanging of iron, all the howling voices in the darkness – I promised myself *never again*. I done with ship.

However, this time round sounded different. I even began to feel excitement creeping up my eight legs. According to the talk, the ship was going to a faraway land called England, though some folks said they were going to the motherland, some said they were going overseas, and some just said, they going 'abroad, man, to work some money.' I must say I liked the sound of abroad, which made me think of the sky's wide blue ceiling. Yes, I fancied the sound of abroad, but even if I were to shape-shift into a spiderman in three-piece suit and trilby hat, or a spiderwoman in frilly cotton frock with matching gloves and high-stepping heels, no way José would I be paying £28.10s for a place on the *Windrush* when I could stow away for free in the ship ceiling in my spider form.

Come departure day, the air was abuzz with the nervous energy that comes with venturing into foreign. But for many of the travellers, faraway England was not that foreign, since many aboard the *Windrush* had once worn the Royal Air Force uniform, only too proud to risk life and limb for old

England. That was during the Second World War, and now the war was over, they felt they'd be returning from Jamaica back to Mother England who'd be waiting with open arms to welcome her overseas sons and daughters to help rebuild war-broken Britain.

As the ship prepared to sail out of Kingston Harbour on that June day of 1948, the scene was all hugs, kisses, waving of handkerchiefs, cries of 'walk good,' and 'don't forget to write soon' and 'send back a photo with de snow and one with de pigeons in Trafalgar Square ...'

And no need to ask if I was there. Foolish question. Of course I was there amidst all the people at the harbourside waving to those on board the ship, and those on board the ship waving back, blowing kisses with one hand and the other hand clinging for dear life to their suitcase.

I thought to myself, About time that I, Anansi, get a piece of this going-to-England action. In nimble-quick time, see me creep along the ship's rail, see me skip stealthy-stealthy onto the nearest wide-brimmed hat, see me shimmy up a rope hanging from a long pole. Soon I, stowaway spider, had well ensconced meself in prime overhead spot for overhead viewing of this Windrushian saga. I thought I'd best keep a low-profile. Just chill out in my vantage point, watching the sea do its thing. Now a shimmering cloth unravelling its blue. Now a dazzling mirror splintering itself into islands, then re-gathering itself into an expanse of turquoise.

'The Gulf of Mexico!' I heard a voice on deck shout.

'Like de ship go make a stop in Mexico,' another voice answered back.

'Where all dem white women and children appear from?'

'Like they coming on board de *Windrush*.'

'Dem don't sound English. Dem a-talk a foreign language.'

'Dem don't sound like Mexican either.'

'Me hear sey dem is Polish.'

'Polish?'

'Dey de lucky ones. When de Russians invaded Poland, dey managed to get out before too late.'

'Their husbands joined up the British army, so they must be can't wait to get back to England and be reunited.'

'De Polish women and dey children boarding, yes.'

Such snatches of talk reaching my ears from the lower deck made me think to myself that this *Windrush* must be a ship of hopes. Maybe the hope of leaving a sunny hurricane-wracked island for a better life in a cold place; maybe the hope of escaping a war-torn land in Eastern Europe and finding refuge elsewhere, even if you can't speak the language; maybe the simple hope of hugging again some loved one who time and tide had put out of arm's reach.

Somewhere along the line, that thing called love must be driving these *Windrush* souls, for I know how that thing called love can make even a coward take a leap of faith into the unknown. And I talking from experience. Once, I myself fell head-over-heels for a young lady by the name of Spark. Oh yes. Spark in name, Spark in nature. She had this way of glowing even in the dark. Who wouldn't want to place a hand around her fluttering yellow waist? Man, she was cuter than cute.

But you know what she do me? Well, hear this. Spark agree to come visit me in she special red dress. 'Her little red number' as she called it. However, she did lay down one condition. I must promise to place a walkway of dry grass leading from her front door right up to my front door.

'Your wish is my command,' I said, giving my best gallant bow.

And all the while my heart beating bongo inside me chest when I spied Spark in the distance, stepping down the dry grass walkway towards my front door – stepping with a crackle and a sizzle. Next thing I know, this selfsame Miss Spark with her little cutey yellow waist, sudden-so she turn one blazing red-raging full-size woman – and all the holler I holler, but Fire ain't stopping, ain't stopping … hellbent for my front door. And crackling up with laugh, she teasing me eardrum with, 'Play with big woman fire, big woman fire burn yu backside!' From that day to today, I learn me lesson. I always keep a respectful distance from Fire.

Then a sudden shout of, 'Bermuda, next stop!' brought me out of my broodings back to now-time. How long we'd be in Bermuda was anybody's guess. So many faces, black and white, from so many lands. All on this one ship. My accent-sharp ears picking up a little twang from Jamaica, Barbados, Trinidad, Guyana. Now faces from Bermuda are boarding the ship of hope to add their little twang to a heap of twang.

From the upper deck I heard a fellow with a posh come-back-from-foreign accent saying how plenty West Indians like himself had fought for King and Country and would be only too happy to take to the skies again and fight for England.

'All for England,' he declared. 'All for the motherland, old chap. After all that English history they drilled into our cranium – 1066 and all that – if I was to bump into Henry the Eighth on Oxford Street, it would be like bumping into an old acquaintance. We know more 'bout English history than the English know themselves. Of course, the colonial education system never breathed a word of African civilisations into the ears of Empire's children – kept us in the dark, all right. Still, they gave us cricket and the English language. My eyes still well up when I recite:

'The boy stood on the burning deck,
Whence all but he had fled;
The flame that lit the battle's wreck,
Shone round him o'er the dead.'

At this point, through the eye-corneas of my eight eyes, I spotted another fellow making a point of slamming down a domino on a table-top as if he had a grievance against that poor table-top.

Turning to the first fellow, the second one laughed and said: 'I never see a daffodil in me born life, yet I coulda recite Wordsworth "Daffodils" in me sleep. So don't bother gimme all dat rhymey-rhymey talk 'bout some boy on some burning deck. You see me? I is a born Trini and I say we calypso is the people's poetry. But de Englishman call we ting folk lyrics and he call he ting de canon. Canon, my ass!'

There was me, thinking a fight was about to break out, but they were soon giving each other a play-play punch as they carried on their man-to-man teasing.

Then, from the lower deck of the ship, my ears picked up the ping-pong sound of a steel pan someone must have brought

along on the journey. As it happened, I spotted a pair of ha
beating a spider steel pan, named after yours truly because the segments chiselled into the old oil drum call to mind the spoke-like pattern of a spider's web.

So it was good to see something of myself mirrored in that drum and to hear a melody spiralling out of old iron towards the hallelujah of a hopeful horizon, for once they'd left their palm-tree islands for uncertain overseas, these *Windrush* souls might have thought they were making this journey on their own. But no, I, their guardian spirit, had lodged myself in the ceiling of their dreams.

'We reach! We reach!' was the chorus at Tilbury docks on that 22 June 1948. And though even the English midsummer was clouded by overhanging grey, I lifted my voice in a praise song remembered from my West African beginnings.

'Who gave word? Who gave word?
Who gave word to hearing?
For hearing to have told Anansi
For Anansi to have told the Creator
For the Creator to have made the things.'

Just then, there was this Windrushian in a trilby hat (his name, I later learned, was Lord Kitchener) breathing in at last the air of the motherland and bursting into song as he stepped off the ship. Not just any song. But a calypso. And the words have stayed with me to this day:

'London is the place for me

London this lovely city
You can go to France or America
India, Asia or Australia
But you must come back to London city ...'

Oh, man, that moment would make the front page. Nothing the front pages like better than a smiling foreigner embracing England's fair shores. But it wasn't all hunky-dory. No Siree! A certain top-notch government official whose name rhymes with bones (all right, to save you guessing, I'll talk out his name – Creech Jones), yes, this selfsame gent, placing his faith in the vagaries of the English weather, assured the Brits not to worry, since these foreigners won't survive three English winters. Yes, the Right Honourable Secretary of State for the Colonies assured the nation that 'once the cold gets the better of them, they'll soon be off, back to their native islands!'

Now, bear with me a moment while I translate into simple Caribbean phraseology what this Mr Creech Jones is really trying to say, which is: 'Once de English frost and sleet freeze off de sunny backsides of these Windrushians, they go hurry back quick-quick to their hurricane islands. Give dem three winters max. Watch dis space ... soon come.'

Poor chap. How was he to know that these Windrushian newcomers and their not-so-new-come second, third, fourth generation, would survive well over seventy winters? Ah well. I, Anansi, could have told him for free: 'Remember the "ship" in "citizenship"!'

Meanwhile, I, Anansi, shuffling unnoticed among the disembarking souls, could sense that despite the doors that will be slammed in their faces, despite the seats on trains and buses that will be left vacant because the locals choose not to sit beside the unfamiliar – yes, despite all that, I knew there and then that my wisdom, my cunning, my at-homeness with the canny (as the Scots would say) would live on in their will to survive.

For whether they be pilot, bus driver, doctor, nurse, midwife, factory worker, musician, writer, teacher, whether their labour be skilled or unskilled, whatever their vocation, I, Anansi, stowaway Spider God, will be the seamstress of their destiny, their tapestry of hopes.

THE BABYHOOD OF COSMOPOLITAN BROWN

1. A Child is Born

Cosmopolitan Brown, first-born of Joshua and Ayesha Brown, arrived into the world, all ten pounds six ounces of him, landing on a waterproof bed-mat, courtesy of a home birth.

It must be said that the young English midwife, experiencing her first encounter of the caul birth kind, was as amazed as the parents at the sight of the little meteor-like head swaddled in a thin grey veil.

'I feel oh-so-so privileged!' she exclaimed, unable to contain her excitement. 'We don't see these often. The amniotic membrane! Meant to be a lucky omen.' With that, she carefully wrapped the caul in clingfilm and laid it like a holy relic on the bedside table.

'Now who's a lucky boy?' the midwife said to the new arrival. 'Born in Mother Nature's designer hoodie!'

And you could say he was the best Christmas present Joshua and Ayesha could ever have hoped for, since he'd arrived on 25 December, a significant day in the Christian calendar.

And though none of the Three Wise Men had followed any star to seaside Brighton where the couple had relocated, that didn't stop Joshua Brown beaming from ear to ear, as he sat there besotted beside Ayesha, both of them over the moon with their baby boy.

'Well, Mrs Brown, looks like we've got us a little Messiah. I'm dead proud of you, luv.'

2. A Good Name is Greater Than Wealth

The exuberant banging of the knocker announced the arrival of Ayesha Brown's mother, up from South London, having received the phone call from her son-in-law, Joshua, that Ayesha had given birth to a baby boy in the wee hours of the morning.

In the flush of fatherhood, he repeated fortissimo, 'A bouncing bundle of joy!'

When told that her grandson's head had emerged garlanded in a caul (the *caput galeatum*, as the Romans would have it), her mum's reaction wasn't quite what they'd been expecting.

'Give thanks! Praise de Lawd!' she exclaimed in her best back-a-yard Jamaican, which she'd resort to in ecstatic moments, the birth of her first grandchild being such a moment. 'Baby born with caul is lucky-lucky baby, destined for greatness.'

Knowing her mother was given to superstitious flights, Ayesha cautioned her: 'Mum, don't you start getting ahead of yourself. It's only the membrane, the amniotic membrane. It won't make the headlines.'

'Blimey!' Joshua burst out in his mid-scrolling and touch-screening. 'It says here, according to good old Wikepedia, that cauls were put up for auction back in Victorian times. Sailors would be queuing up to buy a caul – supposed to protect them from drowning.'

And Ayesha, a big Dickens fan, seemed to remember David Copperfield standing around at the auction of his own caul.

'I'm not about to put our son's caul on eBay!'

Joshua laughed. 'But there's more,' he continued, relishing being the touch-screen bearer of glad tidings. 'Listen to this, guys. It says here caul babies include the likes of Napoleon, Lord Byron, Sigmund Freud, George Formby junior …'

'So he'll be in mixed company,' said new mum Ayesha, smiling at the fleeting vision of a window-cleaning Formby on his famous ukulele.

'I rest my case,' was all her mother said. With that she produced a bottle of white rum from her handbag, sopped the baby's brow then cupped the chubby fist around a silver coin (50p, if you must know), before instructing Joshua and Ayesha to bury the caul.

'Back in Jamaica, I meself quick-time woulda bury de caul under a breadfruit tree to keep dis child grounded in ancestor roots.'

Ayesha reminded her that even Captain Bligh, who had abducted the breadfruit from Tahiti to the West Indies, would be hard-pressed to find a breadfruit tree in the south-east of England. The caul would have to be content with the roots of one of the buddleia trees that seemed intent on taking over their back garden. With a bit of luck, their son's caul might attract as many butterflies as the reputed butterfly bush.

Then, turning to the beaming parents, Ayesha's mum asked: 'What 'bout name for de child?

You two give this consideration? These days people give their children all sort of funny names that the poor pickney have to bear like a cross for de rest of dem life. No true one o' dem Spice Gal name her daughter Bluebell?'

Joshua, who'd always addressed his mother-in-law as 'Mums',

gave a chuckle. 'Well, Mums, we can't leave fancy names only to the celebs, can we now?'

Ayesha's mum sighed. 'I trust to de Good Lord the name Bluebell had nothing to do with the child complexion.'

'Well, we were thinking of Cosmopolitan Brown,' Ayesha said, somehow managing a postnatal blush as she recalled Joshua proposing to her on proverbial bended knee in the grounds of Blenheim Palace, one of the creations of the eighteenth-century landscape architect Capability Brown, who'd apparently come by the nickname from his way of casting a well-considered glance over a stately garden before coming to the conclusion that the garden 'had a great capability for improvement.'

'A great hero of mine,' Joshua, himself a gardener by profession, was quick to emphasise. 'He it was who made me want to take up gardening. And what a name! Capability Brown! So when Ayesha came up out of the blue with Cosmopolitan Brown, the name sort of grew on us, didn't it, babes?'

'Suits a girl as well as a boy,' Ayesha said, chuffed that her husband had remembered to give her the credit for the name.

'Cooosmooopooolitan Brown, I say!' Ayesha's mum declared, doing her impression of a posh English accent. 'Cooosmooopooolitan Brown! Mind you, it will take some getting used to – but a name like Cosmopolitan Brown bound to look impressive on his birth certificate. And like the proverb says, a good name is greater than wealth.'

3. His First Word

And so the new arrival would not only delight the hours of Joshua and Ayesha Brown, but also rob them of much sleep, for Cosmopolitan Brown was a bit of a night person. Just when they thought all was quiet on the nursery front, and just when they'd be about to catch a little snooze, that was precisely the moment he'd be full of beans and ready to boogie in his cot. No amount of cooing and lullabying would sedate him.

Come daytime, he'd be stoned asleep, a totally chilled-out Rip Van Winkle. Such ah-peace-at-last interludes allowed Joshua and Ayesha the luxury of luvvie-duvvie-me-time, even if they were too knackered to partake of anything deeper than cuddles and the caressing of foreheads.

Suddenly, one night, there emerged from the lips of Cosmopolitan Brown what sounded like one amplified syllable: *Ja!*

'Good Lord, Ayesha, did you hear what I just heard? Our son has spoken. I swear he's just uttered his first word – Ja!'

'Sure you didn't hear Ma as in Mama? Or Da as in Dada? Even a possible Ga as in Gaga?'

Despite Ayesha's Babyspeak impression, Joshua would be first to admit he was no expert on the oratorical repertoire of babies. But he'd swear on the grave of his Jewish great-grandfather – the East End bare-knuckle boxer with roots in Lithuania that from the lips of his son had come one well-enunciated:

Ja.

After a repeat performance of the Ja syllable, even Ayesha had to agree that their son's diction could not be faulted, though she'd assumed he'd been trying to say Jack, as just the night before, in a valiant attempt to get the little bugger to sleep, she'd read him *Jack and the Beanstalk*, which met with gurgles of approval.

Ayesha's mum, of course, had an answer for everything – or 'a plaster for every sore' according to the *Concise Oxford Dictionary of Caribbean Usage and Abusage*.

'Just as I thought,' she said. 'This is one blessed caul pickney – and if you sure you hear him cry out JAH, well, that can only mean my grandson must be possessed by the Conquering Lion of the Tribe of Judah.'

But her theory that her grandson would soon be chanting 'Jah Rastafari' had to be ruled out, when Cosmopolitan kept on pointing to the grey tabby kitten – a newly acquired member of their household, for Ayesha had always wanted a cat.

'Ja!' he repeated, loud and clear. Followed by 'Jaguar!' Breaking into the most heart-rending of howls and pointing with a positive finger towards the kitten, as if he'd somehow perceived some purring predator under the playful tabby.

This almost atavistic outburst became so worrying that they decided to return said feline to the pet shop.

4. Enter One Bulldog

It would take a while before Joshua broached the delicate subject of having another go at a pet, this time a dog, Man's reputed best friend.

'I'm not suggesting we get a pit bull terrier or a Rottweiler. No, just a good old child-friendly British bulldog. Like the one in the telly advert. We could always call him Churchill. Even shorten the name to Church. That would be a laugh, won't it? Imagine your mum coming out with something like "Me say a-who de hell you a-bark at, Church?'"

Joshua enjoyed teasing Mums over her churchgoing passion, and his over-the-top impression of her mum's Jamaican accent made Ayesha smile despite her initial misgivings. For she knew the way her Caribbean born-and-bred mum always kept a cautious distance from the canine species. No, she wasn't the kind to get too chummy with a dog. One would have a job convincing Ayesha's mum that a study at a university in Sweden had found dog-kissers to have higher levels of the bonding hormone, oxytocin, and less of the stress hormone, cortisol.

Ayesha had sometimes asked herself why many people she knew with Caribbean roots seem to have a problematic rapport with dogs. Having herself given the subject some academic attention, she thought she might finally have put her finger on the reason behind this suspicion of dogs. Didn't the Conquistadores use dogs to terrify the South American Indians into submission? And on the sugar plantations, wasn't it dogs again that had been used to track down runaway slaves?

Joshua reminded Ayesha that though the Nazis had also used dogs as part of their arsenal, that didn't stop modern Jewish families from keeping a dog for a pet, so you couldn't really generalise about such matters. Besides, he'd always been led to believe that Yahweh had laid down instructions that dogs be rewarded with scraps of meat for keeping quiet. Not letting their barking betray the Exodus out of Egypt.

'Tell you what, babes, we shouldn't let historical baggage stand in the way of adding a little canine to our family unit. A bit of trans-species bonding would do the lad the world of good.'

So, despite her initial iffiness, Ayesha gradually warmed to the idea.

And from a litter advertised at their local pet shop they chose a bulldog. A fawn sable bulldog puppy which Ayesha thought had the most adorable take-me-home eyes, set in a mug of deadpan gloom. Soon a wormed and micro-chipped Churchill was ready for the Browns' household where he immediately fitted in like a glove on four legs.

'Ugly in him face, sweet in him disposition,' was how Ayesha's mum summed up the new arrival. And somehow she managed to restrain her instinctive scepticism. 'I a-bite me tongue,' she said. 'You-all know my opinion of dog!'

Her instinctive scepticism would give way to the pleasure of seeing how her grandson commanded the dog like a precocious dog-whisperer.

'What you two feeding dis child? Look at him calf muscle! Sturdy like one cut-down little man.'

One day, out of the blue, right there in the presence of his grandma, Cosmopolitan Brown toddled across to the dog, stood his ground over its bemused mug, placed one hand inside his little woolly jumper, and said with Emperor-like authority: 'Not tonight, Josephine!'

Pointing a reprimanding finger, he repeated, 'Not tonight, Josephine! *Oh non*, not tonight!'

'What the hell was all *that* about?' Joshua asked, more shaken by the content of the utterance than by the marvel of his son being so incredibly articulate.

Let's be clear about this, dear reader. The average ten-month-old doesn't advance towards a bulldog shouting, 'Not tonight, Josephine!' while the puzzled pet just lies at his heel like a butler patiently awaiting his orders.

Such a scenario convinced Grandma all the more that her caul-baby grandson had been chosen to be a channel of the past: 'Mark my words.'

The proverbial penny dropped when Ayesha swore she'd heard her son speaking to the cowering canine with a French accent. She hesitated to use the word 'abnormal' when 'preternatural' seemed to fit the bill, and by all accounts, preternatural kids are said to be sensitive and possible prodigies.

Joshua smiled when she confided this thought. 'Who knows, babes, we might have a Mozart or Einstein on our hands?'

5. Spot the Prodigy

Ayesha decided to consult the good old *Yellow Pages* for a specialist in child behaviour. A librarian at heart, she preferred the hard-copy feel of the pages, so instead of googling, she flicked through the hefty tome of her preserved *Yellow Pages*, hoping to find 'Caul' listed under the C's. The closest she got to Caul was Cauliflower in an advert for growing your own organic vegetables. But all was not lost. Further down the C's, under Clinics, another advert caught their eyes. *Spot the Prodigy in Your Child.*

Immediately, she got on the phone and made an appointment to see a Dr Simon Saga, an Icelandic therapist who happened to be based in Brighton, just down the road from where Joshua and Ayesha lived in Kingston village, not far from Sussex University where Ayesha worked.

And so they turned up with their prodigy at a basement flat on Seaview Crescent where they were struck as well as amused by the sign beside the doorbell. *Don't abandon hope, all ye who enter here.*

'Looks like this Dr Simon Saga has a dry sense of humour,' Ayesha remarked, keeping one eye on Cosmopolitan who was trying to liberate himself from his pushchair.

As the door opened they were greeted by a tall, well-tanned woman in an Oriental-looking robe, and just beside her left ear, a huge pink rose sprouted from a bed of blond hair. She might just as easily have stepped onto the stage of Glyndebourne Opera House.

Needless to say, Joshua and Ayesha were both taken aback that Dr Simon was in fact a woman, though they were doing their best not to show it.

'I am not surprised you're surprised finding a woman before you. I am oh-so-cross with those *Yellow Pages*. Got my name wrong. Not Simon but Simone – Dr Simone with an e.'

Joshua couldn't help thinking that her voice did exude a certain, how shall we say, grittiness, which was not unappealing, and which he put down to her Icelandic origins.

'Please, come in, do. Would you care for a cup of Thai lemongrass tea, infused with sea moss, or would you rather stay on the straight and narrow with Earl Grey?'

For a moment Joshua thought this might be one of those trick questions like they ask on *Who Wants To Be A Millionaire?* But he decided to take the plunge. 'Thai lemongrass, infused with sea moss would do nicely, if it's no trouble.'

'Same for me, thanks,' Ayesha said. 'Always a first for

everything.'

Just then, Cosmopolitan Brown came out with: 'To tea or not to tea, that is the question.'

'Already I see you are putting your boy to bed with Shakespeare. I'm impressed.'

'More like *Jack and the Beanstalk*,' Ayesha corrected. 'I must say we've never heard him come out with that one before. Definitely not "To tea or not to tea"! We're as surprised as you are, Doctor, aren't we, Josh?'

'That's a new one for me and all,' Joshua agreed. 'What he's been saying, oddly enough, to our pet dog is "Not tonight, Josephine" in this French kinda twang that scares the hell out of Church, I can tell you.'

'Church, did you say?'

'The bulldog pup we got him is named after Churchill in the TV advertisements.'

'"Not tonight, Josephine", your little boy is saying? Are you absolutely sure?'

'Positive.'

Dr Simone Saga's face took on an ecstatic glow, the sort of glow you'd associate with the face of Stephen Hawking on encountering a black hole.

'The signs are clear,' she confided. 'They all point to MAPS.'

'Maps?' Joshua and Ayesha chorused.

'Multiple Aural Possession Syndrome.'

'Now you've lost me,' Joshua said.

'Multiple Aural Possession Syndrome is nowhere near as frightening as it sounds.'

It was a relief to hear there was nothing to fear from MAPS.

'Just a bit of jargon we use in the trade,' Dr Saga reassured them. 'Simply a condition whereby voices from the Other Dimension are possessing a child of this dimension. In the case of your boy, clearly Napoleon is taking him over. Did you know Napoleon was bitten on his wedding night of all nights by the dog belonging to his wife, Empress Josephine? Yes. Since then, Napoleon has had issues with dogs, and is now using your son to channel that anger from beyond the grave.'

Joshua didn't like the sound of that. 'He's just got his first tooth, for Christ's sake! Are you about to suggest anger management?'

'Nothing of the sort.'

But Ayesha too had her concerns. 'So, Doctor, let me get this right. Since our son has Multiple Aural Possession Syndrome, does that mean he'll be keeping us awake at night with a chorus of multi-racial voices?'

'In a word, yes. Did you not hear him break into *Hamlet* a moment ago? "To tea or not to tea!" Speaking through this child are two figures from the past, Shakespeare and Napoleon. A formidable pairing.'

Then, as if to prove the point, Cosmopolitan Brown stood up on his pushchair and declaimed, as to a mass audience: *'I have a dream.'*

Now the therapist sounded even more excited. 'Ah, Dr Martin Luther King is in the driving seat of the boy's personality. Your son is no longer on his pushchair. He is on his mountain top, gazing towards the Promised Land ...'

'Let them eat cake! Let them eat cake!' Cosmopolitan Brown screamed in an all-of-a-sudden falsetto. *'Qu'ils mangent de la brioche!*'

'My French stops at baguette, I'm afraid,' Joshua said, apologising for being monolingual.

'And yet here is your little boy speaking the fluent French of Marie-Antoinette. Anything else I should know?' Dr Saga asked.

'Well, for what it's worth, he was born in a caul,' Ayesha volunteered.

'Splendid. No need to worry. In Romania they are saying that babies born in the caul will be growing up to be vampires. But you know what the Romanians are like. In Poland they are saying a caul baby is born in a bonnet. More – how shall I say – streetwise. Oh, he will be speaking to himself in many voices, and in Iceland we too have a saying: it would be good to have two mouths and speak to yourself with both.'

Then, stroking the chin of Cosmopolitan Brown, she asked: 'So how's our little Einstein doing?'

'Energy equals mass times the speed of light squared!' he screamed at her, rattling the life out of the plastic ducklings on the front of his pushchair.

Dr Saga threw up her arms. 'Did you hear that? Shall we try again? How's our little Einstein doing?'

'Energy equals mass times the speed of light squared,' he responded, this time in a voice of great sorrow.

'Now the boy is repeating Einstein's famous equation. Alas, that equation made the atom bomb possible. Perhaps that is why your son is sounding so sad.'

Nothing, it seemed, would stem the epic flow of tears. You'd think Cosmopolitan Brown was crying his heart out for the entire human race. And all through his bout of weeping, he never once let his attention waver from the violin gleaming above Dr Saga's mantelpiece.

'Sorry, sweetie, that's not a toy,' Ayesha warned, not wanting him to have his own way. But Dr Saga was already passing the instrument to the delighted child.

'Is it expensive?'

'A Stradivarius,' Dr Saga replied. 'Handed down by my father who has gone to the heavens. Can't say the last day it's been played. And did you know that Einstein also played the violin to relax himself after battling with time, space, and motion. If the physicist is, as we speak, possessing him, then your child will take to the violin like a duck to water.'

So said, so done. Cosmopolitan Brown struck the most virtuoso pose a ten-month-old could muster and broke into Beethoven's Kreutzer Sonata. Then, bowing before his invisible audience, he spoke the unexpected words: 'The black man who played the unplayable. Yours truly, George Bridgetower.'

For the first time Dr Saga seemed genuinely puzzled. 'I am recognising the music but the words he is speaking … very strange. Who is this George Bridgetower? Someone you know?'

Ayesha remembered first coming across George Augustus Polgreen Bridgetower while doing research for her dissertation. She smiled as she thought of the look on her then tutor's face when she said she was thinking of entitling her dissertation *Hidden Black History – But Hidden From Whom?*

'Gosh, now all that seems like ages ago. Bridgetower was born in Poland to a Polish mum and a Caribbean dad, John Frederick Bridgetower. John, possibly a freed slave, was fluent in many languages and ended up working for the Austro-

Hungarian court in the late eighteenth century. The couple's son George was a gifted violinist and as a young man he came to England and performed at the Royal Pavilion right here in Brighton.'

Ayesha went on: 'The story goes that the Austrian violinist, Otto Kreutzer, considered Beethoven's sonata to be unplayable. But when George and Beethoven met in Vienna, and Beethoven showed the score to him, Bridgetower took one look and immediately played it back. Beethoven dedicated this sonata to Bridgetower, but later substituted Kreutzer's name after he had a falling-out with George – apparently over a woman. Bridgetower was known as the Abyssinian Prince, and I actually visited his grave at Kensal Rise Cemetery.'

'That would explain why an Afro-European aristocrat from beyond the grave is now speaking through the child,' Dr Saga mused. 'Who knows who will possess him next?'

'God knows,' Joshua sighed.

After a few more virtuoso flourishes, little Cosmopolitan gently returned the Stradivarius to Dr Saga with a gallant nod of the chin, before sitting down in his pushchair. Then, holding onto his bottom, he whispered, 'I stink, therefore I am.'

'Repeat that for me, please, my little man,' said the wide-eyed Dr Saga.

'I stink therefore I am! *Je pue, donc je suis*!'

'Amazing,' Dr Saga concluded. 'Absolutely amazing. Now he is twisting the words of the French philosopher, *René* Descartes, famous for his "I think, therefore I am". In Latin, *cogito, ergo sum*. In French, *Je pense, donc je suis*. How many children, wanting a nappy-change, would say *Je pue, donc je suis*? Mr and

Mrs Brown, you haven't a problem – you have a prodigy.'

'A prodigy?'

'A prodigy,' Dr Saga stressed, laughing. 'But even a prodigy needs a nappy change.'

'In that case,' Ayesha said, 'I'll whisk him to your bathroom, if I may? Won't be long.'

True to her word, Ayesha didn't take long in the bathroom, but long enough to notice a pair of men's boxer shorts and a bottle of aftershave lotion. Joshua couldn't help noticing a peculiar flush of puzzlement on her face.

'Guess we'd better be off. He's had a long day,' was all she said.

'Any special tips, Doctor, for parenting a prodigy?' Joshua chipped in.

'Trust your own instincts. Let the boy be free to talk to the fairies, have conversations with mirrors, tea parties with Mad Hatters. When I was little, I too was talking to the elves. In Iceland we are very big on the elves. A recent poll shows that more than fifty per cent of us Icelanders are believing in the elves. Given a chance, we'd be blaming the elves for climate change. Your son will eventually be outgrowing the voices … such a charming child.'

With their prodigy safely grounded in his car seat, Ayesha turned to Joshua. 'I couldn't help noticing boxer shorts and aftershave lotion in Dr Saga's bathroom.'

'So?'

'Just a thought – whether our Dr Simone might not be Dr Simon after all?'

'You mean transgender like? Flip me! She could have had me fooled. Dr Simone? Dr Simon? It's fine either way. She – he

– gave us solid advice. *Trust your own instincts.*'

And so there they were, like any other family, driving round the rolling Sussex landscape, thinking a spin in the car before going home might help put their prodigy into a more sedative state of mind. In the midst of drifting with the billowing green of the Downs, and gazing at the white chalk cliffs standing like ancient guardians of pagan energy, Cosmopolitan Brown suddenly erupted into a 'Ha-ha,' pointing to an old grey stone wall.

'Say that again, son,' Joshua said, stopping the car.

'Ha-ha wall!'

'Am I missing something?' Ayesha asked.

'Tell you what, sweetheart, already our son is talking about ha-ha walls.'

'What's all this about ha-ha walls?'

'It goes all the way back to the seventeenth century. With a name like ha-ha, you can't blame the lad for thinking it's a funny old wall. Sort of sunken with a ditch to keep cattle away from the gardens. And do you know who used the ha-ha in his designs? Have a guess. None other than Capability Brown.'

Breaking into a grown-up or possessed voice (depending on how you look at it), Cosmopolitan Brown turned to his dad and spoke like a gardener of many years' experience.

'Tell you what, Dad. To master the art of gardening, one must first master the structure of a sentence. A comma to indicate a turn. A dash for a footpath. A full stop in the form of a rockery, or a fish pond to bring the viewer to a sudden halt. An exclamation, creating surprise in the form of a ha-ha wall, perhaps …'

'Wait till his grandma hears what he's been up to,' Ayesha

smiled.

His grandma just gave one of her in-the-know smiles. 'We shall be hearing a lot more from this comeback caul-baby. Watch this space.'

DIALOGUE BETWEEN COD AND CHIP

Cod and a portion of potato chips were lying side by side on the round white moon of a plate when one little chip, unable to bear the silence any longer, suddenly perked up and began to speak. And the conversation went something like this.

Chip: Good morning to you, Cod.

Cod: What's so blooming good about it?

Chip: Oh, dearie me. Some of us have woken up on the wrong side of the plate. Only joking, pal.

Cod: Well, it ain't funny. Can't you read the writing on the wall?

Chip: I see no writing on no wall. What I do see before me is a nice new menu.

Cod: That's exactly what I'm talking about. The writing on your nice new menu. From what it says, things are not looking too good.

Chip: Over the centuries I've been boiled, fried, burnt, wrapped in newspaper … can things get any worse?

Cod: What about me? Haven't I, Cod, had to put up with being filleted, frozen, battered – not to mention being smothered in an avalanche of tomato ketchup.

Chip: Oh, I love when that red stuff comes spurting all over me. It's the closest I'll ever get to having a bath.

Cod: I can tell you obviously haven't read the menu, have you,

Chip?

Chip: Not my job to read the menu.

Cod: Not read the menu? How could you? That's why you're so out of touch. You'll be left behind, Don't tell me you haven't heard that Chicken Tikka Masala has been voted Britain's most popular dish? The people's choice.

Chip: So what's that got to do with me?

Cod: That means me and you both will soon have had our day. We'll be *passé*.

Chip: *Passé*? Nice word. But here's the thing, Cod, I'd have you know that after wheat, maize and rice, I rank fourth in the staple foods of the world.

Cod: Well, your fourth won't mean a thing to Chicken Tikka Masala.

Chip: Who is this Chicken Tikka Masala anyway? The new kid on the block?

Cod: Well, Chicken Tikka Masala has been causing quite a stir, grabbing Brits by the scruff of their tastebuds. Let me tell you how it all started. This guy goes into a Pakistani restaurant in Glasgow and he declares the curry is too dry for his liking. Back in the kitchen, the chef spots a tin of Campbell's tomato soup and gets an idea. Ah, thinks the chef, that will do the job. So he stirs the tomato soup into the curry, followed by a dollop of yoghurt cream. Hey presto! Chicken Tikka Masala is born. The rest, as they say, is history.

Chip: So where's all this leading? Get to the point, Cod.

Cod: I don't know about your ears, but the point is that to my ears Chicken Tikka Masala sounds sort of foreign.

Chip: Foreign, did you say? Doesn't bother me.

Cod: Nothing seems to bother you, Chip.

Chip: Well, for that matter, I'm sort of foreign meself. Just for the record, Cod, my roots go all the way back to the highlands of Peru.

Cod: Do they now?

Chip: All the years we've been mates, not once have you ever asked about my past. Do you know I was French before I was English? My ancestors were the *pommes frites* when they first crossed the Channel and changed their name to potato chips.

Cod: I always thought there was something strange about you, Chip – something sort of foreign.

Chip: Funny you should say that, Cod, because I always thought you were sort of foreign yourself.

Cod: You must be joking. Me, foreign? I, Cod, am English to the bone, down to my pure white flesh, loins and all.

Chip: That's not what I heard from Mushy Peas.

Cod: Mushy Peas like a good gossip. Take everything they say with a pinch of salt or tartar sauce, whatever.

Chip: Sorry, Cod, but I think you'll find that the Norwegians had been preserving your ancestors long before they'd migrated to the English palate. Check your family tree, pal. Bet there's a drop of mighty Viking blood in those pure white loins of yours.

Cod: Mighty Viking blood ... sounds impressive when you put it like that. So let me get this right, Chip. If I'm sort of foreign, and you're sort of foreign, that makes Chicken Tikka Masala one of us. I guess we're all foreign, eh Chip?

Chip: The Atlantic has a lot to answer for.

At that point, their conversation was abruptly interrupted when a pair of hands came to clear away the plate and spread a white tablecloth to welcome the steaming arrival of Chicken Tikka Masala.

Of course, Mushy Peas, observing the proceedings, had to stifle their giggles, while Chicken Korma, feeling a bit jealous of Chicken Tikka Masala, whispered with creamy curry lips, 'I'm going to get you, Chicken Tikka Masala. I'm going to get you – just you wait and see …'

SPICES GOT TALENT

The spices were sitting in rows on the kitchen shelf (as spices do), waiting their turn to be stirred into a casserole, a curry, a gravy, or just waiting to marinate some loin of pork, leg of lamb, or fillet of fish. Yes, there's no denying spices do spend a lot of time just waiting around.

But you must have heard the old proverb that says 'nothing breeds a brainwave like doing nothing'. Well, that's exactly what happened. Chili Pepper got a sudden brainwave. A Eureka moment! To help pass the time, why don't the spices put on a talent show?

Chili Pepper promptly nominated himself the perfect compere for such a show: 'How 'bout we call it *Spices Got Talent*?'

'Sounds good,' agreed his fellow spices.

Chili Pepper, taking his role as compere very seriously, strutted on stage – that is to say, strutted on the pinewood worktop of a brand-new fitted kitchen. And to kick off *Spices Got Talent*, he introduced himself with rapping flair.

'Welcome y'all to Spices Got Talent.
I myself need no fancy intro
'cos I'm the compere with the fiery glow.
Yeah, I'm Chili, the red-hot rover,
ever since that Vasco da Gama,

kidnapped me and took me to Goa.
Yeah, I Chili take the chill out of chill.
Burn, baby, burn, I say burn if you will.
So let's get this show up and running.'

On that note, Purple Garlic, not waiting for Chili to quite finish, rolled onto the stage. You'd think she'd been in showbusiness all her days and all her nights.

'Just call me PG,' said Purple Garlic, showing off her purple glad-rags to the four corners of the kitchen.

'Is that PG as in PG Tips?' Chili teased.

'You know it's PG as in Purple Garlic, and tonight I'll be doing my own composition.'

'That's very brave of you, PG. So what's your number called?'

'"When Garlic Cries" – it's a love song.'

'Best of luck. Take it away, PG.'

Purple Garlic took a deep breath before soaring to operatic heights in more ways than one, for her soprano-like high-C's managed somehow to unsettle the nerves of the high-ceiling chandelier.

'I like the way you peel me.
Chop me, baby, chop me slowly.
Now I'm shrinking in your pot,
Do you think of me? I guess not.

If I promise to lower your cholesterol,
would you cuddle me like a doll?
Or would you retreat as if to say,

"I can smell your breath a mile away.
I can smell your breath a mile away"?'

After Purple Garlic's tear-jerking rendition, there wasn't a dry eye in the house – a dry eye in the kitchen would be more precise. Onion, in particular, feeling goosebumps all over, was keen to let the tears flow. Then Saffron, in skintight leggings with dangly orange threads hanging at the knees, slinked his way centre-stage.

'Well, if it ain't Saffron,' Chili observed.

'The Bard of Saffron, thank you very much!' said Saffron, just to set the record right.

'Thank God it ain't the Bard of Stratford. We could do without those long soliloquies,' said Chili, winking at the audience.

'So, are you ready for my poem?' asked the Bard of Saffron.

'Ready as we'll ever be. In your own time. Take it away, Bard.'

Without further ado, the Bard of Saffron burst into declamatory mode.

'Am I not the Bard of Saffron?
Been around from King Solomon.
Mustard may be keener than keen
and onion doth make an eye weep,
but be warned, forsooth take heed.
A pinch o' me don't come cheap.

'Tumeric, eat your heart out!' Chili muttered under his breath. Tumeric pretended not to hear, while Chili carried on working the audience.

'And now make some noise – give it up for the Nutmeg Trio!'

And with a clatter like the sound of tiny castanets, there appeared three Nutmegs in all their matching finery.

'Looks like a Nutmeg boy band,' said Chili. 'So what song will you three be doing for us tonight?'

'Tonight, Chili, we won't be doing a song. We been there, done that. No, we'll be telling a riddle,' said the Nutmeg Trio in unison.

'We like a bit of guessing, don't we all?' said Chili, giving the trio a red-fingered thumbs-up.

And so with a sway to the left and a sway to the right, the Nutmeg Trio delivered their riddle.

'Thriving under a tropical sky –
riddle me ree, riddle me I.
A lady in a boat drifting
in her redder than red stocking …'

Chili had to admit he hadn't a clue. And in order to give him a hint, the three Nutmegs started rolling around so that Chili could have a better view of their lacy red outer garments.

'Still don't get it? Oh, come on, Chili, make a guess. At this rate we'll be rolling round here all night!'

The penny finally dropped when Chili clocked on to the fact that they must mean the red webbing wrapped around a nutmeg. Their lacy red thingy wasn't exactly his idea of a stocking. But he kept that thought to himself.

'Ah! Think I got it! Silly me! The answer of course is Nutmeg.'

'At last,' sighed the Nutmeg Trio, as they made their exit.

Just then, in wobbled hairy-faced Coconut, looking the worse for wear, as if he could do with a shave.

'Sorry to barge in, guys, but I've got things I need to get off my chest. It pains me when I see my sisteren and bretheren being stoned at a fun fair. Coconut shy! Shy my eye! Human folks ain't shy when it comes to hurling missiles at us coconuts! Not content with desiccating us, they have the cheek to package our juice with some fancy name like pro-biotic.'

Chili, now completely out of his comfort zone, could only think of saying, 'Well, Coconut, you've certainly given us food for thought.'

'But I ain't done,' carried on Coconut in the huskiest of tones. 'I far from done. I say to all you foreign spices, sitting in your cosy corners, time to get off your aromatic arses. How say we plan a mass migration in reverse.'

'Mass migration in reverse?' Chili repeated. 'What's that all about, may I ask?'

'You heard me! Or let me put it another way. I say we repatriate ourselves in reverse.'

'So, let me get this right, Coconut. You saying we spices ought to leg it back to our original home-ground?'

'Couldn't have said it better meself.'

'Coconut, you can't be serious!'

'Do I sound like I'm joking?' Coconut retorted, giving his most fearsome glare, as he'd done back in the eighteenth century when the Portuguese, coming face to face with this hairy fruit, decided to give it the name of Cocos after their hirsute monster who, according to legend, would wait in the shadows in order to scare those children who'd been naughty. At least, that's what parents, at the end of their tether, would tell their tantrum-throwing kids. 'Better behave yourselves or Cocos the bogeyman will come and get you!'

A long silence followed Coconut's outburst before the Nutmeg Trio spoke up as one:

'Coconut may have a point. Besides, we kinda like the sound of migrating in reverse.Any Spice Island is fine by us.'

Then Black Pepper and White Pepper, who'd both shared the same ancestral vine, said they'd be only too happy to relocate to the forests of Malabar.

'I ain't fussed,' said Ginger. 'Wherever I lay my heat, that's my home.'

'Don't know about you lot,' said Purple Garlic, 'but Grandma Garlic always spoke about some faraway place called Egypt where some people called Pharaohs would use us to preserve the dead – "mummies", she called them – so we'll be in good company.'

'Lucky you,' sighed Saffron, 'but I'd have you know my own grandma brought us up to be proud of our family name. And just for the record, Saffron comes from the Arabic for yellow. You lot didn't know that, did you now? So this Bard of Saffron will be migrating back to the East. The Middle will do me.' Then Saffron turned to Coconut. 'So, Coconut, my hairy-faced pal, where do you plan on migrating to in reverse?'

Coconut, who liked to refer to himself as Cocos Nucifera, gave a superior grin. 'None of your business, Saffron. But if you must know, I, Cocos Nucifera, plan on buggering off to a nice sun-blessed beach with blue sea lapping at my feet. Better than being stuck here!'

All of a sudden, there emerged from the depths of a glass jar, a series of pipsqueak noises.

It was the Ginger Biscuits, who hadn't yet got in a word edgewise or any other wise, struggling to express their feelings to Ginger: 'Oh, Ginger, how can we live without you? Please don't go! You'll break our hearts into bits.'

Then a groaning sound filled the freshly painted magnolia-white kitchen with a feeling of deep sadness. Butternut Squash, Marrow, Courgette, Cauliflower, Brussel Sprouts, all used to their wicker-basket residence, were crying with one grief-stricken chorus: 'Oh, Spices, promise you won't ever leave us! We'd all be lost without you …'

ARE YOU SURE YOU ARE IN THE RIGHT PLACE?

Contrary to expectation, Albert Solomon's dream was to be a showjumper and fly the flag for Britain. At his Roman Catholic secondary school in Clapham Junction (postcode Greater London), his P.E. teacher, Mr Bob Beamer, a straight-talking Yorkshireman, had presumed that the lanky Trinidad-born teenager, originating as he did from the West Indies, would naturally gravitate to becoming a fearsome fast bowler. Failing that, perhaps a golden sprinter like that Jamaican fellow, Usain 'Lightning' Bolt.

'Showjumper, did you say? Please don't take this the wrong way, Albert, but how many black people you know own a horse round Clapham Junction?'

Rather than admit to none he could think of, Albert chose to maintain an adolescently ambivalent silence.

Mr Beamer patted him on the shoulder. 'Tell you what, Albert. How say you come and spend a week of the summer hols up Yorkshire way? My sister, Sam, runs her own stables as well as a little guest house. I'll have a word with your parents, shall I?'

'Cool,' replied Albert.

Albert's parents, his dad a policeman, his mum a teacher, agreed that a week in the country would do their son the world of good. But sticklers for West Indian decorum, they reminded

Albert to address Mr Beamer's sister as 'Aunty Samantha' and not 'Sam'. To their way of thinking, 'Sam' would be too familiar. 'Too full-mouth.'

Albert's mum made sure to do him a container of curried goat with roti – a Trini classic she was certain wouldn't be among the delights promised by the Yorkshire moors.

Mr Beamer, a dedicated teacher, even if his methods were sometimes unorthodox, reassured them: 'Your Albert will be in the capable hands of our Sam.'

After what seemed a pastoral eternity in Mr Beamer's old banger, they finally arrived at an arrow pointing to *Sam's Stables*. There to greet them was Mr Beamer's sister. Probably in her late thirties, in jodhpurs, riding boots and jockey-styled helmet over reddish-brown braids.

'Thanks for having me,' Albert said. Then, remembering his mum's instructions, he politely added, 'Aunty Samantha.'

'Aunty Samantha makes me feel old. Just Sam will do. We'd better have you watered and fed.'

'Mum did me some curry goat.'

'No cooking like Mum's cooking, eh? But tomorrow you'll have to try my Sunday roast with real Yorkshire pudding. None of that frozen supermarket crap!'

'Sounds great. But just a cup of tea would be nice, Aunty Samantha.'

With a smile of resignation, she said, 'Ah well, I guess I can get used to being Aunty Samantha. A little politeness goes a long way, Albert. I don't mean to pry, but may I ask how you happened to come by the Biblical name of Solomon?'

No one had ever asked him that question before. Not in so

direct a manner. And Albert with a shy smile explained that his great-grandfather had come from Madeira. 'Mum showed me an old photo in the family album. There was this Portuguese geezer with leather trouser braces, two-toned shoes, handlebar moustache …'

'Sounds like my kind of man. I like them dapper.'

Albert acted as if he hadn't heard: 'From googling Jacob Solomon, I found out my great-grandfather was one of the Sephardic Jews who ended up in Trinidad.'

'Well, never in a month of Sundays would I have imagined that one day I'd be meeting an Afro-Caribbean Brit with a Sephardic Jew in his family tree. Fascinating! King Solomon, of course, was a very wise man, so Albert, you have a lot to live up to.'

Mr Beamer chose that moment to butt in: 'She could talk for England, our Sam. Keep us up all night, given half a chance. But you, Albert, need some early kip. I'll be up with the lark, and so will you, young man. I intend to put you through your paces before Sam takes over. If there's anyone to see you through this showjumping malarkey, our Sam sure can.'

That night, sleep was slow coming. And it wasn't the tea keeping Albert awake. Nor the old attic beams sloping their spooky grin over his bed.

The plain and simple truth was that Albert had never ridden a horse in his life! His closest encounter of the equestrian kind – if you can call it by so grand name – was sitting with his grandmother at the very back of a donkey cart in Port of Spain, Trinidad. Small-boy Albert, squashed in between the market women with their big baskets of fruits, vegetables, ground provision, fish, shrimps, crabs.

Albert had known from doing Latin at school that *equus* meant horse. And the *Roget's Thesaurus* his mum had given him for his thirteenth birthday, also revealed that equinophobia and hippophobia were synonyms, both meaning 'fear of horses'. You'd have thought hippophobia would mean 'fear of hippos'.

Albert switched on the bedside lamp and started flicking through a pile of magazines stacked up in the far corner of the room. A picture on the cover of an old *National Geographic* had caught his eye. It was the picture of a black man in military uniform, waving a sword to the heavens, and seated on a horse.

This monumental figure was in fact Toussaint L'Ouverture, who had led an army of slaves against forces of the Spanish, British and French back in the late eighteenth century on the Caribbean island of Saint Domingue. On 1 January 1804 the island would reclaim its original name Haiti: a Taino word, meaning 'mountainous land'. This was the first Black Republic of the world.

Albert wondered how come he hadn't learned any of that stuff in his sixth-form history class.

He'd learned about Henry VIII and all his beheading ways; about some war called the War of the Roses – and of course that landing of William the Conqueror and his Norman posse at Hastings in 1066.

Not until now was he learning of a slave who could not only read and write, but who'd led a revolution. But what really riveted his attention was the artist's impression of Toussaint L'Ouverture on a horse. If he'd suffered from equinophobia (or hippophobia), how would Toussaint have coped when

Napoleon's troops, mounted on horses, came charging towards him with but one thought on their minds: namely, to reclaim Saint Domingue for the French and return the freed slaves to a life of shackles?

Besides, he wasn't called L'Ouverture for nothing. Legend has it that with his daredevil horsemanship, Toussaint would forge openings in the ranks of the enemy, hence the nickname, L'Ouverture – from *ouvrir*, the French verb 'to open'.

On that night, in that attic room, with somewhere out there the brooding Brontë moors secreting the wuthering haunts of Heathcliff and Cathy, Albert decided to say a silent prayer to Toussaint in order to give himself the strength to overcome his fear of horses and not have to embarrass himself before Mr Beamer and his equestrian sister.

Since the article also stated that Toussaint had been converted to Catholicism, and since Albert himself was a practising Catholic – going to confession and all that – he felt in his heart of hearts that Toussaint would understand the meaning of prayer.

Albert had always been taught to pray to the saints for help. St Anthony was your man to guide you to something you'd lost; St Christopher was there for you when you were about to board an aeroplane (you couldn't leave safety all to the pilot); St Joseph of Cupertino, wherever that was, was the one to turn to for assistance in passing exams – with a little back-up of course from those cod liver oil capsules, which his mum described as 'brain food'. So Albert said a silent prayer to Toussaint L'Ouverture.

That night, Albert dreamed of his great-grandfather Jacob Solomon looking down from a ladder in the clouds and pointing him to a white horse. Albert could feel himself jumping onto the horse then falling … falling … but instead of hitting the ground, he fell into what looked like a billowing hammock.

Next morning, Albert awoke with a spring in his step. He was up with the lark – though he couldn't recall hearing any lark. What he did hear was the alarm on his mobile.

Already outdoors, bright-eyed and bushy-tailed, as the saying goes, there stood Mr Beamer beside a length of rope which he'd fastened between two fence-posts.

'So what's the rope for?' Albert asked.

Mr Beamer smiled: 'The rope, my boy, is for you to limbo under. How can you begin to master the vertical, as in show-jumping, if you haven't first mastered the horizontal, as in limbo?'

Albert shrugged. 'Easy-peasy!'

And with that, arms outstretched, head thrown back, he slithered under the rope, just some eight inches or so off the ground, with such cobra-like ease, you'd think that back in the womb he must have been limbo-ing under his umbilical cord.

Mr Beamer seemed pleased but not overly amazed. 'I knew you had it in you. If you can take to the vertical the way you've taken to the horizontal, tell you what, our Sam will be dead impressed – and talk of the Devil, here she comes!'

Turning to his sister, he said, 'Sam, you've got to see this to believe it! Albert has only gone and taken to limbo like a duck to water. Show Sam your moves. Go on, go for it, lad.'

And again, contorting himself, Houdini-like, Albert made this limbo thing seem a piece of cake.

'Well done, Albert!' Samantha exclaimed from horseback,

holding herself erect. 'I can't wait to see you in the saddle. And there's Flying Snow-Tail at your service, all raring to go.'

With that, she pointed to a white horse which reminded Albert of the one in the dream he'd had the night before.

'Oh, Albert, isn't she adorable? Her mum was a mare of Anglo-Norman bloodline, her dad a thoroughbred Arabian stallion. You can't argue with her pedigree, can you?'

'Awesome!' was all Albert could think of saying. But if truth be told, the lad was, to use an American expression, 'shit scared'. Yet some inner voice kept willing him on to go and make direct eye contact with this Flying Snow-Tail.

Samantha seemed impressed. 'Beautiful, Albert, just beautiful. Do you know that of all the terrestrial animals, horses have the largest eyes?'

'Not just the eyes,' butted in Mr Beamer, winking in her direction. 'Horses are also known to have the largest you-know-what ...'

'Keep it clean, Bob Beamer,' his sister interrupted, playfully flicking her riding whip in his direction. Adding, 'Just ignore him, Albert. He's got a one-track mind. You're doing just fine, so carry on bonding with Flying Snow-Tail.'

Little did she know that Albert had been doing his best to control the stampede of butterflies in his stomach, while Flying Snow-Tail just stood there observing the proceedings, occasionally brushing away a fly, or whatever, with a dismissive swish of her white whisk of a tail.

All of a sudden Albert felt possessed by a kind of weightlessness, as if his legs were obeying some mysterious command greater than his fear, the matter of choice no longer his doing.

Trance-like, yet focused, Albert was soon astride the back of the waiting beast. Something told him to point his shoulder in the direction he'd like the horse to be facing. Flying Snow-Tail promptly responded as if reading Albert's mind. Telepathic, that's the word. Albert found himself and the horse in sync, circling, cantering, counter-cantering, side-stepping. A version of Michael Jackson's moonwalking on four legs.

'Goodness me!' exclaimed Samantha. 'Are you sure Albert has never ridden a horse before?'

'Not in Clapham Junction he hasn't,' Mr Beamer laughed. 'That I can vouch for.'

'You could've had me fooled. Did you see his upward transition – his downward transition? It's almost spooky, the way he's eating up the course with his dressage. Oh, don't you just want to hug him! The boy's a natural.'

And under the guidance of Samantha, who proved as hard a taskmaster as Mr Beamer (a case of up with the lark) Albert not only polished up his newly awakened equestrian talent, but also learned that there was much more to horses than meets the eye. He'd never have guessed that horses' hooves needed moisturising. Or that their muzzle required pre-emptive sun cream, since they too suffered from sunburn. Or that humans weren't the only ones to have a runny nose from hayfever when the pollen count got the better of them.

When Mr Beamer delivered Albert to the door of Mr and Mrs Solomon, the PE teacher was beaming in more than name.

'As you can see, your boy's back in one piece. Albert and Flying Snow-Tail got on like a house on fire. He'll tell you all about it, I'm sure. Anyway, must dash – I'm parked on a double yellow.' And with that, Mr Beamer bangered off in a fanfare of engine-sputtering.

'What's all that about Flying Snow-Tail?' Albert's bemused dad asked.

'Oh, she's a beauty of a filly, Dad. Sired by an Arabian stallion with a mum of Anglo-Norman bloodline, apparently.'

'So since when did Albert Solomon turn jockey?' his dad answered in a dry voice.

'Not jockey, Dad. Equestrian. Aunty Samantha said I could even be a future showjumping Olympian … wicked!'

'And here's me thinking that with your height you could be a future fast bowler for England.'

'You know cricket ain't really my thing, Dad.'

'Cricket is life, son, remember that. I'd always imagined one day I'd be seeing you rubbing a nice red cherry on your lily whites. Not prancing on a horse like you is royalty.' Then, turning in his wife's direction, Albert's dad added, 'This son of yours is a real dark horse – and I don't know why you smiling …'

Albert's mum had indeed been smiling, as she produced an old photo from amongst a pile of newspaper clippings. 'I've been searching heaven and earth for this photo!' she exclaimed, her face almost beatific.

Albert looked – and couldn't believe he was staring at his great-grandfather Jacob Solomon in a Panama hat, posing beside a white horse.

'Oh,' his mum told him, 'your great-grandfather made a fortune out of his rum shop business. Sadly he lost most of it on the horses. Apparently you couldn't keep him away from the race course – so horses must be in your genes, Albert.'

Then Albert's dad, a faint smile shadowing his lips, turned to his son and said, 'Well, boy, this showjumping thing might be your calling, after all. Stick with it – education first and foremost – but stick with it.'

'Cheers, Dad. You heard: in my genes, ain't it?'

Albert Solomon then withdrew, as teenagers do, into the inner sanctum of his room, thinking he'd not bother to mention that silent prayer to Toussaint L'Ouverture. No. That would be their little secret. Horseman to horseman.

True to her promise, and with the right word in the right ear, Samantha would arrange for Albert to be a registered member of a riding club in a leafy London suburb. Albert's sights were well set on the Olympic podium, even though he had to shrug off the odd snide remark from some of his white equestrian mates.

'Hey, Albert! Are you sure you are in the right place?'

MEETING THE BARD

These days I hardly ever venture out from the flat I'd for decades shared with my mum who had always been my rock of ages in my state of self-imposed bachelorhood. God knows what I would have done without my dear mum to see me through that first mental breakdown in my final year at Oxford where the dark clouds had engulfed the silver lining of my studies in Elizabethan Theatre.

Now that Mum is no longer in this world, what is my world but foraging in second-hand bookshops and a round of recurring medication? Except, of course, for the occasional stroll across the Hungerford Bridge. A beautiful spot to view the Thames. Or, alternatively, a beautiful spot to throw oneself into the Thames.

Yet, a feeling of serenity never fails to overcome me as I saunter from one end of that bridge to the other. That is to say, from Embankment Pier towards the Royal Festival Hall. And back again. Does me a world of good, just standing there, observing people heading home fresh from a concert or the theatre, not to mention those so-called normal couples pausing from their cuddling to light up a fag in the misty grey or throw loose change towards some homeless or busking soul.

I recall one moonlit night in the month of April (the cruellest month, if you were to take Eliot's word for it). The night of 23

April 2016, to be precise. The four-hundredth anniversary of the death of none other than the Bard himself.

While crossing the Hungerford, I was suddenly stopped in my tracks by the tootling of an instrument I'd grown to detest. I refer, of course, to the recorder, which for me has become synonymous with memories of my little knuckles being smacked with a 12-inch ruler, a smack from none other than our music teacher, the formidable Mrs Gunnersby, who had zero tolerance for miscreants like myself who dared to chew gum while attempting to master 'Morning Has Broken' on the descant recorder.

When badly played, the recorder (trust me) succeeds in squeaks and shrills designed to drive the ear to the end of whatever tether the human ear happens to possess. But on that April night in question, the said instrument produced such strange and sweet noises that, had I been a sleeping Caliban, I surely would have cried to dream again.

Stranger still, the musician turned out to be a busker in breeches, complete with protuberant codpiece, and bearing an uncanny resemblance to portraits of Shakespeare.

But why am I telling you all this, which is neither here nor there? More to the point, as I drew closer, the man stopped his playing.

'A rollie to spare, good siree?'

I couldn't very well brush him off with 'sorry, don't smoke,' since I myself was at that very moment partaking of a puff, despite the modern tendency these days to regard us smokers as puffing pariahs. An endangered species. So from my pouch I rolled him a rollie and offered a light which he cordially refused, producing his own lighter and adding that he'd run out of baccy. The flame from his lighter haloed a courtly moustache and a pointy Elizabethan beard that made him seem tailor-made to tread the boards of the Globe Theatre.

After emptying my pocket of loose change, I complimented the poor shivering soul on his rendition of what had sounded to me like an Elizabethan jig.

'I've only had four hundred years of practice,' he informed me.

I assumed that he'd been under the influence of an illegal substance. Then I noticed beside him a cardboard sign with the following scribbled in red: *Homeless for my 400th Birthday! How sad is that!*

Forgive me, dear reader, for thinking I just might be in the presence of a nutter, unfortunately one of those words often unkindly directed at the mentally unstable. No, let me rephrase that and say directed at the sensitive, the vulnerable, adrift without the rudder of love amidst the impersonal billows of an insensitive metropolis.

Suddenly, he asked me the date, which I thought rather odd. Normally, a passing stranger would ask of another stranger the time. Why the date?

But before I could reply, he mumbled, 'April the twenty-third, two thousand and sixteen.' Staring straight at me, his thespian profile wreathed in smoke, he asked, 'Ring any bells?'

I reminded him that it was in fact the four-hundredth anniversary of the Bard's death.

'You mean *my* birth and *my* death,' he corrected with the matter-of-factness of someone pointing the way to the nearest tube. 'We all have our entrances and exits, and it's exactly four hundred years to the day since I popped my mortal coil.'

I managed a wry smile at his jumbled metaphor, for he hadn't shuffled off his mortal coil or popped his clogs. No, the fellow before me had managed to kill two birds with one stone by popping his mortal coil! Deciding to humour him, I thought I'd play along with his charade. 'Not often you get the chance to meet Shakespeare in the flesh,' I nodded.

'Slim be the chance indeed though the chances be fat!' he replied. Then, as if to impress upon me that the afterlife hadn't stopped him from keeping abreast of earthly affairs, he said, 'I see I still top the National Curriculum, yet those adolescents fretting their pimples over exams must oft regard my blank verse with blank looks. Oh, pity the poor sods who must ponder my pixies of a *Midsummer Night's Dream*, when they'd rather ponder the pixels of a flat screen. And were I to write an essay on myself, I daresay I would myself fail … flunk … flounder … whatever.'

I informed him that I had read and seen every one of his thirty-seven plays. How, from a seat in the Old Vic, I had seen Cleopatra put that asp to her breast; seen Bottom, a weaver with an ass's head, bewitch Titania, Queen of the Fairies; seen cunning Iago dangle a white handkerchief before the blacked-up face of a bemused Othello.

The fellow didn't seem at all impressed. 'But my sonnets, mate, hast thou read my bleeding sonnets?' he asked in a voice that verged on the threatening.

'All one hundred and fifty-four,' I replied, adding, 'and all in the original folio,' not so much to impress as to carry on humouring him. 'I'm a big, big fan, Willie,' I continued. 'A big, big fan. So much so, there are times I even find myself empathising with that obsessed fan who murdered John Lennon.'

It was only intended as a bit of banter, but the man seemed taken aback when I grabbed him by the shoulder and pulled him towards me.

'Unhand me!' he exclaimed.

Still held in the vice of my grip, close enough for our two breaths to mingle, the pale creature cried out, 'What's your problem, mate? You crazy or what? I'm just an out-of-work actor trying to make a few quid. Posing as the Bard keeps me and the tourists ticking. I'm doing me bit, mate, for the four-hundredth anniversary and all that malarky.'

'All that malarky'? Malarky indeed! Was that how this callow fellow would sum up our son of Stratford-on-Avon, our national treasure, who had bequeathed to us, among his countless gems, the lovely word 'assassination' – a word that takes us back centuries to the Persian Hassan-i Sabbah and his fraternity of assassins.

But was it not the Bard, my beloved Bard – alas, probably rolling in his grave as we speak – who was the first to liberate that exotic word onto the page and stage? How vividly do I recall a dillydallying Macbeth (Act 1 Scene 7) willing himself to get the bloody deed over and be done with:

'If it were done when 'tis done, then 'twere well
it were done quickly; if the assassination
could trammel up the consequence, and catch
with his surcease success;'

And there and then, assassination returned to ring its ghostly bells in the temple of my grey matter. My head was now a blizzard of voices instructing me to assassinate – yes, assassinate – this recorder-tootling impostor standing before me, this pretender to the throne of the Bard; voices instructing me to slay the villain on the Hungerford Bridge as Othello had slain the Ottoman on the Rialto.

But not until I'd returned home did it dawn upon me that without my mother there to remind me, I had failed to take my medication on the day in question. A lapse of memory that could have had dire consequences, for without my medication I am capable of the unspeakable. Unable, as the Bard would put it, to make a conquest of myself.

And to this day, I keep asking myself: did I accost an apparition? Or was I the accosted?

CARPE NOCTEM

The Professor was a man of formidable intellectual stamina and sartorial elegance, not averse to dyeing his goatee to match the colour of whatever jacket he happened to be wearing.

Among the Professor's dilettante achievements was a self-published cookbook, *Cooking Asian with a Caucasian*, which would take fusion food to a whole new level. His gastronomic innovations included Victorian sponge with a sprinkling of curry powder, and rhubarb scones with a drizzle of Devonshire clotted cream and hot Madras sauce.

After his culinary phase had worn off, the Professor went on to propose to the BBC the idea of a reality TV series, *The Great British Shake-Off*, showcasing competing canines being doused by a super-powered barrage of water. The waterlogged dogs would then proceed to shake off the intrusive element. The dog that managed to shake off its wetness in the fastest time would be declared the winner, and *The Great British Shake-Off* trophy – in the form of a beautiful cut-glass bone – would be awarded to the owner of the victorious dog. A prestigious adornment for over the mantelpiece.

Needless to say, his proposal was considered 'loony' by the BBC Controller. Besides, Animal Rights activists might not take kindly to the idea of little Jack Russells, cuddly poodles, not to mention royal corgis, having to submit on prime-time TV to a vicious premeditated onslaught of water – Noah's nemesis.

An insatiable writer of erudite letters to the press, and always courting controversy, even for the sake of being contrary – wearing a green nose for Red Nose Day, for instance – the Professor was famous for once stirring things up on the TV programme *Question Time* by pulling up the interviewer, Mr Jonathan Axman, for making repeated reference to 'carpe diem' (seize the day).

Cutting an upright dapper figure amidst the tierly-seated audience, our Professor said his piece in no uncertain terms: 'With all due respect to the Roman poet, Horace, to whom the expression *carpe diem* is attributed, when people like you, Mr Axman, carp on (pun intended) about *carpe diem*, aren't you forgetting something? Whatever happened to *carpe noctem*? That's right. Seize the night. In the interest of fair-play between black and white, doesn't the night deserve a look-in? How about *carpe noctem*? Would make a nice change, don't you think?

'So the question I'd like to put to you, Mr Axman, is this: are you prey to the primeval association of darkness with fear? A fear transferred to races of darker pigment?'

A group of women in the audience immediately applauded his interjection with an almost Dionysian gusto.

'Good on you, Professor!' they screamed in chorus. 'About time we seized the night! *Carpe noctem! Carpe noctem!*'

Mr Axman apologised profusely to the viewers for the unforeseen outburst of oestrogen, explaining that they represented the militant group SNTPP (Say No To Poxy Patriarchy), whose manifesto highlighted the demonisation of the dark and listed a series of historical crimes committed in the name of light.

Just then, amidst a flurry of gestures and gasps, the Professor collapsed. Motionless. Sadly, little did those millions of viewers glued to the screen realise that they were, in fact, witnessing the Professor's final breath. For when the now prostrate Professor began mumbling, 'Carpe noctem,' with foaming lips and bodily contortions, they assumed this was all part of the act. A dramatic aside, in a manner of speaking.

But no, what they'd been witnessing was reality TV at its most heart-rendingly real.

Our Professor was dead.

Even when Mr Axman threw up his arms and uttered, 'My God! It appears the Professor is no longer in possession of a pulse!' the proverbial penny still hadn't dropped.

All was finally made clear when the women of Say No To Poxy Patriarchy all began ululating, that is to say, expressing their grief with acoustic abandon.

One of the following day's tabloids, reporting the passing of the Professor, headlined the story in the boldest of typeface: **THE LAST OF THE LOONIES!**

The article went on to say that the belated Professor had been a maverick scholar with a 'tendency to bend over black-ward'.

At his funeral, his female supporters from the SNTPP could be heard chanting, 'Carpe noctem,' a cappella style. And as a mark of respect to the Professor, they also ensured that his ecologically friendly coffin was not despatched without being duly garlanded in florist-designed, hand-crafted bouquets of black-dyed roses.

BLOW THAT HORN FOR KING AND COUNTRY!

King Henry VIII decides to call an emergency meeting at Hampton Court. A sort of Tudor equivalent of what Number 10 calls 'a high-level COBRA meeting, chaired by the Prime Minister'.

Of course, the modern version lacks the medieval fanfare of trumpets and fluttering banners, and what passes for a coffee break in today's Houses of Parliament would pale in comparison, gastronomically speaking, with the obese Henry's buffet-style spread of meats: from rabbit, goose, swan and pheasant to canapés of venison shot by noble huntsmen in the King's very own deer parks. What's more, those emergency meetings, chaired by King Henry himself, were far removed from the modern notion of brainstorming. Henry scoffed at words such as 'brainstorming' and 'team-player', as they say in the corporate world.

'Brainstorming is for pussy footers,' to quote King Henry. 'I'll be done with team-playing ditherers.'

And true enough, the King's word was the rule of law, and his minions knew only too well that it was better to be a yes-man with your neck intact, than stand up to the King and be another of the headless ones. Indeed, had T.S. Eliot been crossing London Bridge on that summery morning of 6 July 1535, the poet would have got the full import of his line: *I had not thought death had undone so many* – for there among the undone would be none other than the spiked head of the King's trusted adviser, Sir Thomas More. The author of *Utopia* could never have dreamed he'd meet such an *un*-Utopian end.

Even two of the King's six wives would, in fact, end up on his royal hit-list. Anne Boleyn, his second wife, and her feisty cousin Catherine Howard, his fourth wife, would both lose their heads to the executioner's axe in the must-see tourist attraction known as the Tower of London.

Fortunately, the business of beheading would not be on today's agenda at Henry's court. There was the more pressing matter arising out of the Minutes – namely the erection of a monument to celebrate John Blanke, the King's black trumpeter whose name, by a twist of irony, was rooted in the French word *blanc*, meaning white.

To tell the truth, King Henry would have preferred John Blanke to have been blessed with a more appropriate English surname. 'What's wrong with simple John White, for crying out loud?' Every time he uttered the name Blanke, the King would rankle still at the memory of England's old enemy across the Channel. The bloody French!

To banish this linguistic salt from an old wound, Henry would resort to his Welsh roots by affectionately calling John Blanke by the name of John-o Boy-o.

The King would say, for example, 'By royal command, John-o Boy-o, blow that horn for King and Country. Regale mine ear with a riff or two, as you did for my old man, Henry the Seventh.'

And John Blanke would put his trumpet to his lips and let

his black ancestors do the rest.

Sometimes the King, who liked dressing up, would don a turban in the manner of a Sultan and have a private jam session with his favourite Moor-complexioned trumpeter. As turbaned Henry tootled 'Greensleeves' on his recorder, John Blanke would improvise, filling in the gaps in a muted Miles Davis sort of register, not wanting to disrespectfully drown out the King's warbling descant.

Among the King's treasured keepsakes was the letter written by John Blanke to His Majesty. Diplomatically couched and impeccably quilled, that letter was, in fact, demanding not only a pay rise but promotion to a position left vacant after the untimely demise of Dominic Justinian, an Italian trumpeter.

The cheek of John-o Boy-o! Henry thought to himself. I like a man with balls!

And the King would smile to himself whenever he perused John Blanke's letter, which is now preserved in the National Archives:

To the King, Our Sovereign Lord,

In most humble wise beseecheth Your Highness, your true and faithful servant John Blanke, one of your trumpets. That whereas his wage now and as yet is not sufficient to maintain and keep him to do Your Grace like service as other your trumpets do. It may therefore please Your Highness in consideration of the true and faithful service which your servant daily doeth unto Your Grace and so during his life intendeth to do, to give and grant unto him the same room (position) of Trumpet which Dominic deceased late had ...

Can a King refuse such a well-worded petition? thought King Henry to himself. Besides, didn't this same John Blanke play at his dad's funeral and again at his own Coronation?

Henry's signature would guarantee that John Blanke's request be met, livery, board and lodging paid for out of the royal treasury.

But the icing on the cake would turn out to be a little surprise in the form of a statue to be erected in tribute to John Blanke.

'How about a statue of pure alabaster, my lord of lords?' suggested one of King Henry's Right Honourable arse-lickers.

The King scowled. 'John Blanke may be white by name, but alabaster becomes his complexion not one jot.'

'How about a statue of ebony, Your Most Gracious Grace?' suggested another Right Honourable arse-licker.

The King scowled again.'John Blanke may be black but ebony doth overstate the case. Neither alabaster nor ebony doth hit the mark.'

'How about a statue made of salt?' suggested his Jester-in-Residence, otherwise known as Phipp the Fool.

Now, what you should know is that professional Fools were employed by Renaissance monarchs as a way of maintaining their royal sanity. And Henry was very fond of his Fool. 'A statue of salt?' he said, smiling. 'Fool, you do have your Eureka moments! Your folly is the fodder that maketh my day. What would I do without you, Fool? A statue of salt it shall be.'

And so said, so done.

Soon, out of salt quarried from the mines of Chester, the

Master Craftsman of the Royal Household had carved a statue in tribute to John Blanke. There he was, as real as flesh and blood, the African trumpeter, gorgeously attired, mounted on a horse, trumpet to his lips, all fashioned out of salt.

A miracle of craftsmanship!

And the King was most pleased that John Blanke was pleased.

'Salt keepeth away evil spirits,' smiled the African trumpeter.

Of course, come the first rains, the miracle of craftsmanship was washed away. Returned to the elements.

There are, however, a number of scholars who to this day dispute that such a statue had ever existed. They maintain that while there is pictorial evidence of a turbaned black trumpeter in the Westminster Tournament Roll, no records pertaining to a statue of salt are to be found anywhere in the royal archives, the British Library, the Bodleian Library, or for that matter, Wikipedia.

Yet one Japanese tourist swears on the grave of his Sumo-wrestling grandfather that on a visit to Hampton Court, he had seen with his own two eyes the ghost of a black man mounted on a horse that melted in the pouring rain. And to prove his point, the Japanese tourist (who shall be nameless) managed to record for posterity on his mobile the poem he'd heard coming from the mouth of the aforementioned ghost:

In Norman French the name has a ring that's nice.
Not John Blanke, Jean Blanc, to be precise.
Shall we say a Tudor gentleman of colour?
Or one who brought colour to the Tudor court?

What's in a name leaves ample room to ponder
for am I not John White the Black
and Black John White rolled into one turban?
In days when the Henrys ruled the royal roost
and the King himself took to the manly joust
I hailed the thrust of lance with trumpet blast.
I, the equestrian exotic of the retinue,
blowing for every pence of my shillings' due.

Thus the North African winds had followed me
to an England known both as Olde and Merrie.
Yes, I whose Moorish skin echoed midnight's sky,
surveyed from a turban's rainbow my adopted Albion,
and to those white cliffs my lips put forth their clarion.
Not quite a fanfare for diversity,
simply doing my bit for pomp and pageantry.
Yet when history's footnotes begin to grow more bold
and the heart's tapestry unrolls its spectrum,
hear again my trumpet's dark notes rising out of vellum.

SPIRIT OF RUM

One-eyed. One-armed. Handicapped was what many might have said of Admiral Lord Horatio Nelson in those days when tough-talking seamen weren't exactly politically correct. Back then they didn't think of saying 'physically challenged'. And as the Admiral, shot in the shoulder by a French sniper, lay dying on his flagship, the HMS *Victory*, his hardened, politically incorrect crew would express their sentiments in words to this effect:

Ole One-eyed don't look too good.
Where he's going, he won't be needing his one good eye.
Looks like we're losing Ole One-armed.
Ole One-armed won't be needing that one good arm neither.

In whatever terms they couched their impending loss, the one thing they all agreed on was the need to preserve the Admiral's corpse for a big send-off, one worthy of someone who'd suffered from seasickness all his naval life yet went on to show the French who was boss of Trafalgar.

Besides, how often do you meet a Norfolk bloke who's lost one arm in Santa Cruz, one eye in Corsica, and becomes a legend on a monumental column that draws tourists like flies to honey? Or maybe a moth to flame. Please yourself.

And what better way to preserve such an Admiral than in a barrel of booze?

One school of thought suggests that the choice was a cask of French brandy. There was something of a poetic irony or poetic justice in the Admiral's lifeless limbs being preserved for the journey to Gibraltar en route to London in nothing less than brandy, courtesy of his old enemy, *les Français*.

So how do I know all this stuff? That's because I was there: an eye-witness as well as a mouth-witness. For I am the spirit of Rum. You heard me. I repeat: *Rum*. The legitimate offspring of that bitter-sweet bastard, Sugar. And I can testify that the chosen tipple to preserve Nelson's corpse was in fact rum. Yes, a barrel of my golden-brown self.

Not for nothing that to this day I bear the nickname, 'Nelson's blood'. Of course, I prefer my other nickname, Kill-Devil, which has a certain ring to it, a directness that keeps me in the good company of the Horny One. Saccharum may hint at Latin origin. Rumbouillon may add a splash of French. Both a little too highfalutin' for my taste. So let's stick with that one no-nonsense syllable: *Rum*.

I, the nectar to put the totter in a stride, the slurp in a tongue, the glaze in an eye, the fire-water that makes the cheeks of tourist-white-man out-pink the pink of a hibiscus flower. Whatever your race or creed, remember I am also the river that flows steady-steady, winding my course past those treacherous cubes of ice, to the red sea of your blood to flood the dam of your brains.

Not to be confused with gin or vodka, in my transparent guise, I play my role in libation to the unseen. Pour me in the corners of that new house you move into so that bad vibes may move out.

Pour me at that graveside so that the departed may be quenched.

Pour me to welcome that baby. Sop that newborn brow with white me that the child may walk good into the future.

I, Rum, who would take Europe's palate by storm, was known to entice many a galleon to a watery end, and many a skull and crossbone have perished for a gallon of my liquid gold, not to mention those ancestral limbs scattered to the Atlantic like broken fetishes.

But despite that Middle Passage shadow, I know when and where and how to lighten up. To chill.

Take, for example, Christmas-time, when black cake comes into its own. Oh, makes your mouth water, just thinking of that West Indian spin on English fruitcake. That's when I don't mind playing second fiddle to the marzipan, the pitted cherries, the ground almonds, the whatnot.

But I warning you upfront. Don't be deceived by the moreish taste. Don't underestimate my invisible presence in the black cake. Take one slice too many, and you so tipsy, you could find yourself flat on your face under the mistletoe.

And if your idea of Paradise is lying prone on sunny white sands with a cocktail in your hand, then I only too happy to be the hot-buttered additive to your coconut soufflé.

But I does feel to wince deep down in my golden-brown heart, when you choose to drown me in Coca-Cola. If you must weaken me, well, that's up to you. Add a little coconut water, I don't mind.

But I draw the bloody line at Ribena. When you fire a rum, I say fire straight.

You know what I does find pleasing to my soul? When I, Rum, become the fuel of a little romance. Like the time (coming back to Nelson), yes, like the time I witnessed the Admiral himself in a cosy one-to-one with Mrs Frances Nisbet, a young not-so-short-of-cash widow. When he wasn't 1000 feet above sealevel, high up there on Saddle Hill at his look-out fortress, keeping his good eye glued to his spyglass for any sign of the French, our boy Nelson, sporting a long hippy-style ponytail, would be knocking back Nelson's blood, breezing out on Mrs Nisbet's veranda, watching the fireflies making tiny galaxies of themselves in the trembling Nevis twilight. And so from a cut-glass tumbler into which I'd been poured, complete with loud ice, I would observe the Admiral courting this widow whom he called 'my Fanny'.

Yes, I was there at the courtship, and yes, I was there when Nelson and his Fanny tied the knot at Montpelier plantation on that March day of 1787. And for the record, it was at Montpelier plantation that an ox, intended for the wedding feast, was getting fatter and fatter in a specially prepared pen. But on the night before the wedding, as the gods would have it, some hungry slaves stumbled upon the well-fat beast. Since roasted ox wasn't part of the slave menu, I can't say I blame these runaway souls for tucking in. (Waste not want not. God don't come, He does send.)

Some would call this an inauspicious start to married life, for a little pigeon later told me that Nelson had been two-timing his Fanny with some outside woman by the name of

Emma Hamilton. The same Fanny with whom he'd chilled out on a West Indian veranda, the same Fanny who had nursed him back to health after the Admiral had succeeded in getting that left arm blown off.

What Nelson do is Nelson's business. I, Rum, cast no stone. Content to be my silent golden-brown self, minding my own business in a cut-glass tumbler. Or was it crystal? Don't bother me.

What does bother me is when I flash back to that letter Nelson wrote in 1809. I know because I was there in my usual cut-glass position right next to the inkwell while the man was busy putting pen to paper, thinking he was alone.

In that letter Nelson declared himself a 'firm friend of the colonial system'. His words, not mine. He went on to express disapproval of Wilberforce and the Abolitionists. Their free-the-slaves doctrine was one he considered 'cursed and damned!'

That was the moment I began to understand why Nelson's column in Trafalgar Square is standing so high, the dead Admiral now in command of the London skyline. And the reason Nelson is towering way up there is so tourists will have to strain their neck, or bend over backwards like they dancing limbo, in order to see for themselves whether a national hero has feet carved of stone or feet carved of clay.

Now I'll leave you one parting thought for the road. Pour a glass of me and lift history to your lips.

GRANDMA PIGEON

Grandma Pigeon liked nothing better than making speeches. Yes, her brood of pigeon grandchildren could tell you a thing or two about their grandma's legendary fondness for speechifying. At the last family gathering, after a dinner of sunflower seeds, Grandma Pigeon even recited a poem.

Reciting a poem at a private family get-together is nowhere near as nerve-wracking as making a speech in public, but this is exactly what Grandma Pigeon had to prepare herself for. Soon she would be the key-note speaker for the Confederation of Omnipresent Pigeons, better known as COOP. Attending the convention would be red-billed pigeons, white-headed pigeons, spotty-winged pigeons, even green pigeons from Japan and pink pigeons from the island of Mauritius. Visiting delegations of foreign pigeons were expected to fly in for the big occasion. But mostly, there would be grey wood pigeons from around Britain and across Europe.

It was as if the pigeons of the world had been keeping a diary and weren't going to miss the date for anything.

At last the day of the pigeon confederation arrived, and Grandma Pigeon had every intention of rising to the occasion. She'd made sure she had practised her speech in anticipation of that moment, 'Please welcome to the stage … live and direct … Grandma Pigeon!'

The time had come for Grandma Pigeon to clear her throat, tilt back a sip of water, puff out her chest:

'Sister Pigeons, Brother Pigeons, as spokes-pigeon for COOP, I thank you all for joining us here at Trafalgar Square for our annual Confederation of Omnipresent Pigeons (COOP). Delighted to see so many of you – and I'd like us to give a warm welcome to our sisters and brothers who flew in from Australia in the wee hours of the morning. I trust our visitors from kookaburra country will make the most of the strawberry season.

'Now, let's get straight down to matters of concern to the pigeon population. Word has got around our pigeon grapevine that humans are plotting to eliminate us from their city centres. In the past they've tried scaring us off with their fake falcons and fake hawks, but trust me: what I say ain't fake news. Grandma Pigeon doesn't do fake news.'

At this point, the gathering of pigeons responded with a flapping of wings. Grandma Pigeon had them eating out of her hands, or to be more precise, eating out of her claws.

'We pigeons have survived traps, guns, poisoned seed and newfangled hi-tech contraptions. Yet we pigeons are still here. We pigeons haven't gone the way of our dear departed Dodo. And why do humans have it in for us? Well, you've heard it all before. How we make a mess of their city centres. How we pollute their office buildings. Do humans really expect us to take them seriously, when they're only too ready to throw any old rubbish to any old where, even chuck their plastic into the sea?

'Now, what I'm about to say will surely tickle you all. This is rich, very rich. Imagine humans referring to us pigeons as "flying rats"!'

This comment sent the confederation into a flurry of stitches.

'Told you you'd be tickled,' Grandma remarked. 'When first I heard the expression, flying rats, I myself laughed so much I thought my throat would lose its puff. Flying rats indeed! Do I look like I have a shoelace for a tail?' she asked, displaying her fine fan-shaped tail-bottom.

Then, deciding to milk the moment, Grandma gave an almighty coo. 'Is that a squeak?' she enquired. 'Unless I'm going deaf, sounds like a coo to me. Poor humans! Can't tell their squeaks from their coos. And do we pigeons settle for some dusty hole in a house of humans? Most certainly not. Not when there are city centres up for grabs!

'But more to the point,' Grandma Pigeon went on more quietly, 'what would lonely senior citizens on a park bench do without us to feed and keep them company? No disrespect, but ducks can be so boring. Same old, same old. We bring an element of surprise. Maybe swooping down on an unsuspecting sandwich. Or even depositing (for luck) a dropping or two on a head unfortunate enough to be without hat or umbrella.'

More wing-flapping and chest-puffing followed. Then a collective outburst of coo-coo-coos that the noise of London buses and taxis couldn't drown out.

'Humans have such short memories. Do we need to remind them that we were to the Romans what mobile phones are to modern humans? Do we need to remind them of how we braved the winds and raining bullets to carry messages to far-flung corners of the planet, though our wings were wounded, our feathers frayed? This was during World War One – or was it World War Two? Humans make so many wars, we pigeons can't keep track.

'And when that Nelson triumphed at Trafalgar, who was it that delivered the news? A pigeon, of course. So humans shouldn't be so shocked to find us perched on the Admiral's head. Dropping pigeon graffiti all over his person is just our pigeon way of passive resistance. Dove has always had the limelight but we pigeons are also birds of peace.

'So hear me, Oh all you members of COOP. Let us continue in the tradition of our comrade pigeons who squat on the grand piazzas of Venice and who get comfy on that famous cathedral of Paris, not to mention the squares of Amsterdam, Athens, Rome and other cities further afield that time doesn't permit me to mention. Nothing will stop us making our voices heard! No. Our coos will not be silenced.

'So, let us give London tourists something to write home about. Humans are saying they want their city back. We say, "Have your city back." But we plan to take back control of the rooftops, the piazzas, the church steeples, the pavements. And do you know why? Because they belong to us. Pigeons.'

At that point in the proceedings, Grandma Pigeon received a flapping ovation.

SAVE SOME BACK FOR BLACK ANNIS

How Whitman O'Sullivan, a black Barbadian, had come by the Irish surname, O'Sullivan, was all down to a certain Oliver Cromwell, otherwise known in Gaelic circles as simply 'that bastard'. For it was by the orders of the self-styled Lord Protector that many an indentured Irish and Scot had been shipped off at gunpoint in the mid-seventeenth century from colonised Ireland to colonised Barbados.

'The curse of Cromwell be upon you' gained the status of an expletive and the noun Barbados would morph into the verb Barbadosed – to be Barbadosed becoming the round-about-speak for penal transplantation from the familiar shores of the Shannon and the Clyde to the sun-beaten hell of an overseas plantation.

It was only a matter of time before the blistering heat of Barbados had turned the pale legs under their kilts the colour of beetroot. Hence they'd come to be known by the pejorative nickname of Red Legs. But since the human species seems more at ease with always having some other to look down on, the newly arrived Red Legs would look down on the freed slaves who would in turn look down on the Red Legs as 'de poor white from under de hill'.

The long and short of this historical palaver is that there's more to the O'Sullivan family tree than meets the eye. As for the

Whitman, that was all down to his father, Everton O'Sullivan (may he rest in peace) persuading his mother, Edna O'Sullivan (may she also rest in peace) that the name Whitman O'Sullivan had a certain ring to it. Plus there was the small matter of his father keeping by his bedside to his dying day a well-thumbed copy of Walt Whitman's *Leaves of Grass* next to an equally well-thumbed copy of the Bible.

After a session of Guinness and Mount Gay rum – not necessarily in that order – the old boy was always up for a good argument, and should anyone dare accuse him of contradicting himself, he'd declare in a strong Bajan accent, quoting from Whitman, 'Cor blimey, man, I contain multitudes.' He'd also make a similar declaration after slamming down a domino hard enough to unbalance the Formica-top table that had somehow managed to stand the test of time.

Whitman O'Sullivan heard, from his deathbed father the following words: 'Boy, I ain't got long. Remember, son, Barbados is our born-ground little England, but Africa in we blood, same way Ireland in we blood.

Always remember you're an O'Sullivan. Our family tree contains multitudes – you don't need me, my boy, to tell you that. When I gone, promise to scatter some of my ashes under the old breadfruit tree where my navel-string bury, but save back some for Black Annis ...'

And with those last words – *save back some for Black Annis* – the old boy was gone.

The mention of Black Annis, however, made Whitman O'Sullivan think immediately of his grandmother, the departed Anna O'Sullivan, whom everybody knew fondly as 'Black Annie'.

But one day, going through his dad's stuff, he just happened to stumble on an old occult magazine where the headline of one article caught his eye: BLACK ANNIS – THE SHINING ONE.

According to the article, Black Annis was a Goddess of Rebirth, one of the Celtic spinners of the thread of life, etymologically connected to the Earth Mother, Anu, whom the Saxons later demonised as Black Annis. Those Saxons have a lot to answer for, thought Whitman O'Sullivan, as he went on to read that a pair of neighbouring mountains near Killarney were named after the breasts of the selfsame goddess. Apparently, come the summer solstice, visitors would flock like pilgrims to mount the 'Paps of Anu' as the twin peaks are called, and place the offering of a stone on the cairns that tower for metres above.

Whitman O'Sullivan couldn't help smiling to himself when he observed how his father, true to his colonial drilling in Latin, had neatly pencilled *nota bene* instead of *note well* in the margin beside the Paps of Anu and the reference to Black Annis.

Though Whitman O'Sullivan wasn't into all that occult stuff, the thought occurred to him that his father must have been looking over his shoulder and guiding him to the article. 'Synchronicity strikes again,' as his father would say when strange things happened. Black Annis, Whitman concluded, must be a clue to the site in Ireland where his dad had asked for some of his ashes to be scattered.

And so, fast forward to our man, Whitman O'Sullivan, at this moment seated in the Leprechaun's Arms, a little-known pub somewhere on the Emerald Isle. In the briefcase at his side sits the silver urn bearing what's left of his father. He's decided that if you were going to meet with Black Annis, what better than a dark brew to psych yourself up. And the solitary blackbird pecking at the leftovers on the tables out in the garden of the Leprechaun's Arms also seems to augur well.

'You're not from round these parts, are you?' says one of the locals in a plaid trilby, staring across his pint of – you've guessed it – the dark brew.

'No,' replies Whitman O'Sullivan. 'I've just come with some ashes.'

The man perks up: 'You've come with some hashish? Well, I'll be damned. The Good Lord doesn't come but He sends, all right. For here am I, dying for a smoke, when lo and behold like a genie outta bottle in walks a darkie fellow bearing the good tidings of some hashish.'

Obviously, the man had got the wrong end of the stick. And some might consider his last remark even somewhat politically incorrect. But Whitman O'Sullivan has a good laugh, having prepared himself for what's stereotypically called the Irish gift of the gab. In fact, he would have been disappointed if he'd encountered a cold silence in the Leprechaun's Arms.

'So, what's all the laughter about?' the man asks.

'It's funny because I meant I've come with some *ashes*,' Whitman O'Sullivan repeats.

'Oh, I get you – ashes, did you say? How silly of me! And what would a fellow like yourself be doing walking around with ashes, if you don't mind my asking?'

'It's my father's ashes. Live and direct from Bridgetown, Barbados.'

'How old was he?' the man asks.

'Just short of ninety.'

'Well, that's a fine innings, all right. Must be the rum – they sure know how to make rum out there in Barbados. Mind you, they been practising for centuries … but they don't produce fast bowlers like they used to. Back in the day they'd give the English a right old hammering. Never thought I'd live to see the day even our Irish lads would clobber England at cricket! Would you believe it?'

Whitman O'Sullivan smiles. "Well, not for nothing is it called the game of glorious uncertainty.'

'I'm more of a rugby man meself. By the way, the name's Fionn O'Sullivan – and to whom do I have the very great pleasure of speaking?'

'Whitman O'Sullivan,' our man replies in a somewhat bemused tone.

'Holy Mary, Mother of God!' the man exclaims. 'A white O'Sullivan and a black O'Sullivan, all in the one room! That bastard Cromwell must be rolling in his grave! But tell me, does the name Seamus O'Sullivan ring any bells?'

Whitman O'Sullivan recalls how his dad once showed him a photo in the family album and said the person in the photo was his great-great-grandfather whose name was in fact Seamus O'Sullivan.

The man laughs and takes a swig of his Guinness.'Well, I'll be damned! I've heard tell of a certain Seamus O'Sullivan who ended up in Barbados. Couldn't keep his meat and two veg to himself, not that Seamus O'Sullivan. Fathered children all over the island – had a bit of a sweet eye for the black ladies from what me ma told me. And what with Barbados being such a tiny island, you won't have to travel far to sow your wild oats.

Never been there meself, mind you, but me ma always spoke of distant relations somewhere out in Barbados.'

At that point Whitman O'Sullivan, our seeker of Black Annis, promptly takes out his mobile and displays on the screen some old family photos, including the faded one of a Seamus O'Sullivan along with one of his dad, mum and paternal grandmother whom everyone called Black Annie.

'That's the one – the very one!' the man exclaims when he sees the photo of Seamus O'Sullivan. 'Be Jaysus! That's our Seamus O'Sullivan, all right. So what it all boils down to is one simple fact: looks like you and me must have the same old devil, Seamus O'Sullivan, hiding somewhere up our family tree. And so, tell me now, is your grandmother the one they called Black Annie? Let's have another look at her … quite a looker, ain't she? And may the fairies take me tongue if I tell a lie when I say your Black Annie is the spitting image of me own ma, and she's as white as they come. Now ain't that something?'

'It's a small world,' says Whitman O'Sullivan, adding with a nod of the head, 'Genes can't hide.'

'A small world indeed, I do believe. And as one O'Sullivan to another, allow me to buy you a drink,' the man says.

'Just a half, thanks,' Whitman O'Sullivan replies.

'I'll have you know, only half a man drinks half a pint.'

'On second thoughts, let me get you a drink,' offers Whitman O'Sullivan, about to head for the bar.

'For God's sake,' the man insists, 'keep your money in your pocket. Just sit yourself down. After all, you're the one who's come a mighty long way. Get another pint of the dark stuff down ya, then you can hand me all the lowdown on the long-lost O'Sullivans of Barbados.' Winking at Whitman O'Sullivan, he adds: 'And don't you be sparing me all the sordid details.'

'Well, Fionn, looks like me and you, we have a heap of history to catch up on. How much time have you got?'

'Oh, don't you worry, I've got all the time in the world – and time, as they say, is a great storyteller. You did say, didn't you, that you'd brought along your dad's ashes all the way from Barbados? Well, look on the bright side, without those ashes, tell me now and in the name of God, what are the chances of a black and a white O'Sullivan meeting in the Leprechaun's Arms of all places?'

'Synchronicity strikes again, as my dad used to say …'

And so, to put an end to this tale, the two well-met O'Sullivans agreed to trek the path together to the Paps of Anu and cast the ashes of another O'Sullivan to the colourless winds.

THE HATS AND THE HATS-NOT

In a certain town the men all wore hats. In another town, a stone's throw to the west, the men there all went about hatless. One was known as Hats Town, the other as Hatless Town.

Hats Town boasted hats to suit every whim –
panamas of fine straw, fedoras with snappy brim,
top hats of slinky silk worn at a stylish tilt,
hats of fur, hats of leather, hats for every weather.

Some of the men of Hats Town even went to bed
with sporty panamas over striped pyjamas,
which made, they say, their sleep so much calmer.
And at a ceremony known as Hatting the Head,

Hats Town boys (only the boys, it must be said)
were presented, on entering their teens,
with a brand-new dapper bowler or trilby
amidst much feasting and making merry.

'Not fair, not fair!' cried Hats Town girls, enraged.
'How come we don't get hats when we come of age?'
But such was the ancient custom of Hats Town,
and so it had been for many a generation.

Now, in Hatless Town, life was very different.
Hats were as foreign as spices from the Orient.
Hats in Hatless Town were nowhere to be seen,
except on the head of Hatless Town's Lord Mayor.

His towering top hat with buckle glinting
was, to put it mildly, most eye-catching.
A top hat designed (according to rumour)
to stop the bullet of any assassin.

The Lord Mayor, known for his sense of humour,
addressed Hatless Town in this manner:
'Let Hats Town folk fool themselves they're superior
by sleeping in panamas and reaping in fedoras.

Hats off to you, Oh hatless men of Hatless Town,
you who bare your brave heads to the rain and sun.
Hatless we have been from the days of yore,
hatless we shall be till the cows fail to come home!'

'But I see you stand not hatless among the hatless,'
chimed in Clown-Woman, last of the female clowns.
'Well spotted, Clown-Woman,' the Lord Mayor replied,
displaying his top hat that dwarfed a king's crown.

'But as your Lord Mayor of Hatless Town,
I am duty bound to make an impression.
I did consider a bowler, a trilby, a sombrero,
but a top hat, you'll agree, makes more of a show.'

But Clown-Woman wasn't short of an opinion.
'So what about the hatless women of Hatless Town?
Do we not bare our brave heads to the rain and sun?
What if we refuse to tend the harvest hatless?'

Clown-Woman was one known for stirring up unrest.
Her question met with female applause,
which made the Lord Mayor pause.
There and then he proposed a new law.

'Clown-Woman has indeed spoken wisely,'
the Lord Mayor of Hatless Town agreed.
'So from this day, the women of Hatless Town
shall go forth in hats of all descriptions.'

'What about the girls?' Clown-Woman asked,
showing off her teenaged granddaughter.
A sprightly sapling in her grandma's gaze.
A lean-upon walking stick in her twilight years.

'I hadn't thought of that, Clown-Woman,'
the Mayor replied. 'Well, better late than never!
But there's no reason, no reason whatsoever
why Hatless Town girls, on entering their teens,

shouldn't have their heads adorned like queens
in a ceremony we shall call Hatting the Hatless.
We'll show Hats Town that we are their betters.
Come on, ladies, bring on the ostrich feathers!'

'And what about us men who herd the cattle?'
the Chief of the herdsmen interrupted.
'Must we the herdsmen graze our cows hatless,
while the women harvest in fancy headdress?'

'Very well,' said the Lord Mayor. 'Have it your way.
Let the heads of men and boys rejoice in hats.
In fact, let all of Hatless Town, whatever gender or age,
begin wearing hats topped with dazzling plumage.'

Just then, a shot sounded! From out of nowhere
a bullet headed for the Lord Mayor's headwear.
Luckily, he was saved by that golden buckle
and shrugged off the incident with a chuckle.

The people of Hatless Town cried: 'A miracle!'
And to this day, in Hatless Town's market square,
there for all to view is that marvel of a buckle
displayed with the Mayor's top hat in a case of glass.

And like pilgrims shrouded in a reverential air
folk from far and wide would file past.
Some even bowed their heads as a mark of respect
to that buckle that had foiled an assassin's bullet.

Of course, the men of Hats Town (old rivals to the west)
were none too pleased when they heard the news
that Hatless Town folk no longer walked hatless.
Even their women now sported hats of many hues.

So just to be different, Hats Town passed a new law,
forbidding hats; all Hats Town folk were required
to cast their beloved hats on a public bonfire
where the finest of fedoras turned to embers.

Anyone from Hats Town caught in possession of a hat
would be liable to arrest and possible incarceration.
That's how Hats Town came to be called Hatless Town.
And from then on, Hatless Town was renamed Hats Town.

As for Clown-Woman, she carried on wisely clowning.
And her granddaughter followed in her footsteps.
Yes, to her granddaughter (as stated in her will)
Clown-Woman left her fool's cap with shining bells.

PIG TALK

The community of pigs was not the slightest bit amused when they got word from across the Pond that North American street slang for the police was 'pigs'. The pigs were quick to take offence at the comparison and considered it politically incorrect, if not downright offensive, to describe the police in terms of pigs.

To refer to the boys in blue as Babylon wasn't too bad. Babylon, after all, was an ancient civilisation known for its Hanging Gardens. But when North Americans start equating the police with pigs, well, that was taking liberties worthy of a lawsuit. A linguistic slur not to be taken lightly.

The time has come for the community of pigs to call an emergency meeting. First to speak is Papa Curly Tail, the most senior member of SOP (Seniority of Pigs). Papa Curly Tail – or Papa CT as he prefers to be called – begins by going down memory lane, all the way back in time to the long-long-long-ago when a goddess by the name of SOW (Source of Wallowing) had chosen, out of all the creatures, a pig's back on which to give birth.

Papa CT then goes on to remind the assembly of pigs of their famous great-great-great-great-great-great-grandfather Boar, better known as GAB (Great Ancestor Boar), whose mighty bristles had filled the ancient Celts with courage and spurred on the Vikings to hop in their longboats and head bravely for

England.

'Oh yes, fellow pigs, lend me an ear,' Papa CT declaims in his most pigatorical tone of voice. 'Our ancestor's bristles, lest you forget, once adorned the helmets of warriors. Boar bristles were once treasured like the relics of Saints. And just for the record, it was none other than our great-great-great-great-great-great-grandmother CCP (Clever-Clogs Pig) who, when she was just a wee piggy, managed to outwit that Mr Wolf by building her house not out of flammable cladding, or silly sticks and straw, but out of reinforced redbrick. The rest is fairytale history: when that Mr Wolf made his way down the chimney, there was a nice big cauldron of hot water waiting to give him a sizzling welcome – as in a boiling death down to his chinny-chin-chin.'

Hearing how Clever-Clogs Pig had undone Mr Wolf never failed to fill the pigs with a sense of pride in their ancestry. But knowing that Papa CT was prone to rambling on, Mama Pinky the rapping pig, known for speaking her mind in rhyme, decides to butt in. And here's Mama Pinky in full flow:

'Respect to you, Papa T
but pay heed to Mama P
now ain't time to be
dwelling on past glory
we know our history
we're pigs, dig it
mud's our habit
mud keeps us fit
yeah, guys, bring it on
bring on the mud

humans don't know
what they're missing
but when they call cops pigs
it's us pigs they're dissin'
but we pigs don't wield no baton
so they can stick their cops
right up their bacon
we pigs we're on their case
we done sussed the double talkin'
human race ...'

The pigs unanimously grunt their approval of the way Mama Pinky had delivered their grievance with such musicality. The more militant pigs snort to the heavens and stamp their feet in the mud. In the mood for extreme action.

Whatever it takes.

All the commotion brings good Farmer Briggs squelching through the mud in his wellies. A peace-loving man, he'd been farming all his life, like his father and grandfather before him. Farmer Briggs loved his pigs and even turned to them for guidance about the weather. If his pigs were rolling in the dust or munching straw, he'd take this as a sure sign of rain to come. Farmer Briggs was even bi-lingual, so to speak, for he went to great lengths to master Pig talk.

'Oink! Oink!' he yells at them. 'So tell me, my darling gruntlings, what's all this hullabaloo about?'

Papa Curly Tail, as elder of the porcine fraternity, takes Farmer Briggs to one side and explains the situation. After hearing Papa CT's version of this unprecedented state of affairs,

Farmer Briggs, deep in thought, begins to imagine the worst case scenario.

If the pigs were opposed to the idea of the police being referred to as pigs, what if the cows were to get it into their heads to start objecting to humans calling a stupid person 'silly cow'?

What if the sheep should take offence at sheep being used to describe humans who go around following the herd? What if the chickens were to get into a huff every time humans point to a coward and cry 'Chicken'?

And, God forbid, what if the rats were to raise a right hoo-ha every time a cheating lover had been called a 'dirty rat'?

Farmer Briggs shudders at the thought of having a tooth-and-claw uprising on his hands. He imagines his beloved pigs storming the Police Department – the way that mob stormed Capitol Hill in Washington. In order to divert such a crisis, he decides to go down on his hands and knees, wallowing in the mud, thinking that the delicacy of the situation called for getting down diplomatically to the level of the pigs for the purpose of equal eye contact.

Then, with a series of well-orchestrated snorts and grunts, Farmer Briggs, choosing his words ever so carefully, says to the pigs that animals shouldn't really make generalisations about humans.

Since pigs don't really get the hang of abstractions, the pigs just gaze at him, nonplussed.

So, in order to break down the human concept of generalisations, Farmer Briggs points to the village policeman in the distance, stoically pedalling his bike like a postman up a cobbled country lane.

'Now, Pigs, take a good look at that nice policeman struggling uphill, doing his duty, never complaining. Isn't he the very one who rescued many a kitten stuck up a tree? Doesn't that policeman put a smile on the face of many an old lady when he retrieves her kitten in one piece? Yea or nay?'

No reply. Except for Mama Pinky, who gives a sceptical snort and turns her rear end towards Farmer Briggs. He chooses to ignore her and carry on speaking.

'As I was saying, before I was so rudely interrupted, I take it all you pigs would agree that the aforementioned policeman is jolly nice? So when humans, especially the young, shout "Pigs!" at the police, what they really mean to say is that the Police are jolly nice – friendly, and very intelligent, just like you pigs are jolly nice – friendly, and very intelligent. Humans are, in fact, paying you pigs a compliment. Do you see my point? Oink if you do.'

At first the pigs don't look too convinced by his line of reasoning, but they hold Farmer Briggs in such high esteem, they trust in his word. So they oink agreement and carry on being jolly pigs.

That went rather well, thinks Farmer Briggs, once the ordeal is over. But he stays awake at night, thinking that such a diplomatic approach might not work with the rats.

SECURITY

Once there was a security guard who stood outside a supermarket. Duty-bound and muscle-bound, he'd stand in position. See him there, clean-shaven gleaming scalp, earring in one ear, a tattooed tarantula spinning its green web on the side of his neck.

Not the sort of man you might care to mess with, judging by his looks and stance. But ever so eager to fetch the odd trolley for a senior citizen. Every so often he'd stop someone from entering the supermarket without a safety mask on, not in these testing times, more likely apocalyptic times, when the un-hugged can be driven to the edge.

Sometimes, in his line of duty, he'd have reason to gently but firmly move on the homeless girl with the well-fed dog at her side, begging loose change at the entrance to buy-one-get-one-free.

Yet, in between all the humdrum to-ing and fro-ing of trolleys, the security guard would seize a quiet moment to move across to the plants displayed outside and promptly put to rights any pot that had fallen or been disarranged.

Now what's that tomato doing among the lavender? the security guard would be thinking to himself. And what's that pot of rosemary doing lying on its side? The same goes for that pot of basil. Must be the wind – unless some customer had perhaps knocked it over and couldn't be bothered to put it back where it belongs.

And why in the name of God is that pot of bay leaf among the piles of slug pellets, organic compost and the premium houseplant potting mix? And just look at that: some idiot has gone and stubbed out a cigarette in the pot of lovely salvias, would you believe it?

People don't seem to care much these days. But plants are different. He's never had reason to grapple with a plant for shoplifting. Plants don't carry knives.

Once he has restored the horizontal to the vertical, the security guard returns to his position.

There he is right now, standing, not quite as rigid as those figures in Madame Tussaud's Wax Museum. Some say our Bob (as he's called) is a simple man and most likely suffering from some sort of compulsive disorder. 'Everything in its right place' seems to be his inner obsessive mantra.

Or so they think. For what his colleagues don't know is that the security guard is only doing this job in order to put food on the table. Family means the world to him.

If truth be told, his secret lifelong dream was to be a gardener. To create an oasis of calm in the core of frenzy.

WHAT'S IN A NAME?

Esther Silverstein, eager to get away from the bustle of London, couldn't wait to move in with her two cats to the small cottage she'd bought in leafy Elderberryville. To be honest, Esther had never even heard of the place until a bit of googling set that right. But no prizes for guessing how it came to be called Elderberryville.

Surrounded by sprawling acres of elderberry trees with their clusters of creamy five-pointed petals that turn to a firmament of dark autumnal purple, seemed just the sort of place where Esther could switch off and at last buckle down to that novel she'd been dreaming of writing for ages.

Just over an hour's drive into the big city, far enough to be away from the stress, yet close enough to slip down for her once-a-week adult beginners' class in Hebrew at a synagogue in North London. That would take care of Wednesday evenings. Maybe she'd allow a couple of days for teaching yoga, which she was qualified to do. She couldn't promise to be guru to those Elderberryville residents aspiring to self-mastery (or self-mistressdom as the case may be), but at least her yogic contortions might save some soul from the threshold of obesity.

That sounded to Esther like Plan A. That way she'd have ample me-time to do battle with the blank page and spend some quality time with Esau and Jacob.

In case you're wondering who Esau and Jacob could be, well, rest assured, dear reader, these two are neither son nor husband, for Esther is neither married nor a mother. Neither chick nor child, as the saying goes. Esau and Jacob are her two feline friends. More than friends – more like soulmates. Her two munchkins. A unique breed she'd managed to acquire from a breeder after a long waiting list.

'They're from the same litter,' the breeder had informed her. 'So you could say they're twins, I guess. Not identical, of course.'

For Esther Silverstein it was love at first purr! And the moment she'd heard they were twins, her mind flashed instantly to those twin brothers, Esau and Jacob, and to that Biblical depiction of Esau as a man of hair and Jacob as a man of smoothness.

One kitten grabbed her attention by flaunting at her ankle a fountain of reddish fur that almost covered his shorter-than-usual legs. Nor was he backward in coming forward to smooch her instep, to-ing and fro-ing his tongue like a caressing pendulum.

The other kitten wasn't quite so pushy. And more of a cinnamon-coloured, chubby-legged munchkin with dreamy walnut-y eyes. And certainly not quite as furry and hairy as his brother.

That day, Esther knew she'd be homeward bound with a special addition to her household in the form of Esau and Jacob who would still be there for her in her cottage in Elderberryville as they'd been there for her in her North London studio flat.

Being a multi-tasker with a method to her madness, Esther thought she'd keep a cat journal with little jottings on Esau and Jacob. Their personality traits. Their quirks. Their little misdemeanours.

How purr-fectly adorable! she wrote in her journal. Who gives a toss if it's an overworked pun? How short-sighted of that prophet Isaiah who dissed cats as 'demons of the desert'. Why couldn't Isaiah follow the example of the prophet Muhammad (bless him) who, according to legend, rather than disturb the slumber of his beloved cat, Muezza, all cosied up on the sleeve of his coat, cushion beside him, the prophet opted for cutting off the sleeve.

How about that for tender loving care?

Having shorter legs than your regular cat proved challenging to the twins, especially when, motivated by the smell of marinating fish, they'd attempt to hurdle the kitchen worktop. But those short legs would prove advantageous in other respects. My God, you should see them dart at full speed straight through the narrow gap below the futon in Esther's living room without even having to duck or arch their backs.

A pair of limbo dancers disguised in fur, is what she'd scribbled in her cat journal.

From the start, Esau seemed more of the outdoor type. Like his namesake, he was one for open spaces. To ferret out a mouse in the garden was his idea of fun.

Jacob, on the other hand, was more of your indoor type. A homestead boy like his namesake. There was nothing Jacob liked more than sitting beside Esther on the sofa and boxing her paperclips onto the floor.

And when Esther went into yoga mode, both cats would join her on her yoga mat, overlooked by a wooden carving she'd picked up from an antique shop. A carving of no less than the Egyptian cat-goddess, Bast, seated on a scarab. As if that wasn't enough, Esau and Jacob, in imitation of Esther, would attain unorthodox yogic postures that would make even an orthodox Hindu yogi more than proud.

As for calisthenic grace, eat your heart out, you Eastern European gymnasts, to quote again from her cat journal. But what particularly caught Esther's notice was their way of taking turns at playfully mounting each other, which she took to be a case of boys will be boys. A bout of wrestling wouldn't do any harm. In fact, some laddish wrestling would help prepare them for any potentially ferocious encounter with any bully of an alpha-male tomcat who thinks he's boss of the hood.

What Esther had taken for a bit of boyish play, however, soon grew into amorous proportions. So she decided to consult her much-thumbed copy of *Catlore* by Desmond Morris, her favourite English zoologist who also happened to be a surrealist painter with a penchant for observing the Naked Ape, otherwise known as Homo Sapiens. With credentials like that behind him, Esther had no reason not to trust in Dr Morris who had this to say:

If two male or two female cats find themselves together, sexually aroused but lacking suitable mates, one member of the pair may suddenly switch to the mating pattern of the other sex ...

So that's what the wrestling was all about, thought Esther. Esau and Jacob might be gay cats, or bi-sexual? Certainly, flexibly non-binary.

Once she came home to find them both a little on the poorly side. Esau wasn't his usual frisky self. And Jacob was laid back beyond the horizontal. Why this sudden redness of the lips? Why the retching on the carpet? Oh, you poor things! Then Esther spotted the source of their discomfort – a toad struggling to find an exit to the patio, having escaped with a few minor bruises. Or, to be more to the point, spat out with feline gastronomical distaste!

More than likely, Esau, true to his predatory nature, must have sussed out the toad's hide-out in the garden, sunk his fangs into the ill-fated creature that for him happened to be in the right place at the right time, then dragged his conquest indoors, where his brother Jacob must have had a nibble as you might do a pizza delivered straight to your door.

So the next stop for Esther was the Elderberryville vet, Dr Jason Beckham, known for his homeopathic treatments for pets. One feature of Dr Beckham's clinic which Esther thought odd, though charming in its own way, was the ritual of the young lady at the front desk, announcing with the ebullience of a fresh-faced intern, for the benefit of all in the waiting room, the name of the ailing pet in conjunction with that of its owner. This meant that a Rover Smith was followed by a Lassie Watson followed by a Rex Jones.

But what brings a smile to Esther's lips is when an old lady in a woollen beret, and bearing a parrot in a cage, leaps forward to the announcement of 'Polly O'Connell'.

Soon comes the moment for Esau and Jacob Silverstein, as announced by the receptionist.

The pet-lovers biding their turn in the waiting room give eyebrow-raised glances as Esther Silverstein strides from her seat with her beloved Esau and Jacob towards the presence of Dr Jason Beckham, a well-kept sixty or so, still sporting a rockstar-styled head of blond hair.

Dr Beckham begins by putting Esther at her ease, enquiring whether she was related to the Silversteins who'd been neighbours to the Beckhams back in Berlin back in the day. Esther says she couldn't be sure but she'd heard her grandmother speak of a famous gynaecologist by the name of Dr Beckham who'd actually delivered her as a baby.

'Small world,' Dr Beckham smiles. 'Synchronicity, according to that Swiss Dr Carl Jung. For what would you say if I told you I'm the grandson of Dr Beckham, and I've heard my own grandmother speak of their neighbours, the Silversteins?'

'Small world,' Esther agrees.

For Esau and Jacob, the vet prescribes a course of garlic oil capsules, which he assures Esther would act as a natural antibiotic.

Suddenly, just on the point of leaving, Esther blurts out: 'Tell me, Dr Beckham, are there gay cats?'

Dr Beckham smiles, pointing a biro in her direction. 'You'd be surprised how liberal and liberated our four-footed friends can be. Not just bi-sexual but tri-sexual, meaning they'll try anything.'

'I'll bear that in mind, Dr Beckham. And I'll also keep an eye on next door's dog, just in case Esau and Jacob should decide to go trans-species.'

On that note, they shake hands, and Dr Beckham also high-fives Esau and Jacob by the paw.

All goes clockwork-smooth for the next couple of weeks, with Esau and Jacob occupying each other and allowing Esther

her own space to get on with that novel. Then, one day Esther gets a scare when Esau and Jacob suddenly go missing.

She is just about to scan in a mugshot of Esau and Jacob, and run off some Missing Munchkin leaflets to hand around the neighbourhood, when there's a knock at the door. Before her stands a bespectacled young man, probably in his late twenties, mild-mannered yet oozing confidence. Teutonic-tall, he could have been a tenor out of a Wagner opera.

'I am returning your munchkins. I am your new next-door neighbour and I found them hiding in my garden shed,' he said, cradling Esau and Jacob in his arms and enunciating every word with a metronomic precision. 'And here they are. Drop-dead gorgeous, they are, and they seem to have … how you say in English – *the hots* for my little Jack.'

'Is Jack your son?' Esther asks.

For some reason her question throws the young man into fits of laughter. 'So funny! No, Jack is my dog. My little Jack Russell.'

'Yes, very funny,' Esther replies. 'Thanks for returning my munchkins in one piece. So, you've already been introduced to my Esau and Jacob?'

'Maximillian Fassbinder, no relation to Fassbinder the German film-maker. Just call me Max. And your name, please?'

'Esther Silverstein. '

'A pleasure to meet you, Esther.'

'So, Max, what brings you to Elderberryville?'

'I am here to finish my dissertation. Ornithology is my thing. When I am saying to my English friends in the pub that I am here to study the English birds, they are laughing always …

I wanted somewhere not too far from London but far enough for me to be close to the birds. Elderberryville sounded perfect for finding nesting places for many kinds of birds – finches, orioles, warblers, tanagers. And the pigeons, they are oh-so loving to eat the elderberries. Yester evening down by the river I am seeing a kingfisher trying to chew off more than he can bite. I apologise, Esther. You must excuse my English.'

'No, you're doing fine. My German stops at Schnapps!'

'And if you don't mind my prying … are you married? Single?'

'I most certainly am single,' Esther answers, surprised to hear herself speaking more slowly than usual and delivering each word with emphasis.

'Me too,' says Max. 'The single dad of a little Jack.' With that, Maximilian Fassbinder strides off into the evening of late September's Indian summer, the rear of his denims making its presence perkily palpable.

Later that night, as she brushes out the tangles in her dark mane, Esther Silverstein smiles to herself, letting the decade or so age difference between herself and her ornithologist neighbour slip through her thoughts like a bar of luxury soap. And in that basking moment, she even thinks up a title for her still-gestating novel. Yes, the working title she decides for now would be *The Munchkin Matchmaker.*

Esau and Jacob, needless to say, purred their literary approval.

SMITH & SMITH

There was this village, Tweedham-on-Twee, cradled by charming views of the River Twee. On the old church perched a weathercock that watched over the village like an ancient sentinel. And in this village of Tweedham-on-Twee, there lived a blacksmith whose father before him had been a blacksmith. As far back as he could remember, his white ancestors had been blacksmiths. The thought made him smile, for somehow he couldn't imagine a black blacksmith.

'Blackie' as he was fondly called by the village folk, had never travelled beyond his village. Tweedham-on-Twee was all he knew. His life was his hammer and anvil, and the village faces as familiar to him as the horses he shod. Sometimes though, alone with his bellows and forge, he would talk to himself for company, and even swear at the world around him. It was then the thought of getting married would cross his mind.

One day, a black woman arrived in the village amidst much curiosity. Hair braided, skin shining, she asked the first person she met, 'Is this the village of Tweedham-on-Twee?'

'Sure as my name is Thatcher,' replied the man, whose father before him had been a thatcher. 'Tweedham-on-Twee it is, Tweedham-on-Twee it shall ever be. And what's a foreign lady like you be doing in these parts?'

The woman answered that she was a travelling blacksmith

in search of work.

Of course, the villagers, who by now had gathered round, were all gaping in surprise. They had never seen a woman blacksmith, or a black blacksmith, never mind a black woman blacksmith.

'Never rains but it pours,' declared Mr Thatcher, the thatcher, who saw himself as the village spokesman. 'Let's take our visitor to our own blacksmith and see if she be telling the truth.

Black woman blacksmith indeed!'

So off they went to their blacksmith's cottage at the edge of the village. But when they knocked there was no reply. Blackie's hammer was strangely silent. Inside, they found the blacksmith just sitting on his bench. He had on his usual leather apron but work seemed farthest from his mind. The forge fire was dwindling, and Blackie just sat there, a pale shadow of himself.

'Work, work, work,' he said, shaking his head. 'All I ever do is work, bleeding work. Today I'm in no mood to lift me flipping hammer. It's one o' them days.'

'Well,' said Mr Thatcher the thatcher, 'here's a lady looking for work. A foreign lady, I might add. A travelling black blacksmith!'

Blackie, the white blacksmith, looked at the black woman who said she was also a blacksmith and he almost pinched himself. Could this be happening in Tweedham-on-Twee?

Blackie actually found himself blushing.

'Can you, good lady, shoe a horse?' was all he said.

'*Shoo* a horse yes, *shoe* a horse never!' quipped Mr Thatcher the thatcher, laughing at his own joke. Then, winking at Mr Cobbler the cobbler, he said, 'How say she shoe that horse in the field just off the old Roman road?'

The villagers laughed because they knew he could only mean the white horse that roamed at night and that nobody dared go near – not since the cobbler's wife, Mrs Cobbler, who was always seeing things, swore she had seen a headless Roman with sword and all, riding that same white horse.

'That horse will test her shoeing all right,' said Mr Thatcher the thatcher, pointing the visitor towards a footpath that led past a stream and into the woods. Pleased with himself, he said aside to the other villagers: 'I'd say we handled that rather well. A dozen like her couldn't shoe that devil of a horse. And she's bound to get lost. Something tells me we've just seen the last of our black woman "blacksmith".'

And so the black woman blacksmith kept on down the path, past the stream, over a little bridge, until she came to the field just off the old Roman road. There, haunches to the wind, stood a horse as white as Albion's chalky hills.

She took one look at the horse and thought, A bit low in the heel. Then she walked straight up to the animal like an old friend and whispered in its ear:

'Seven the days of the week.
Seven the colours of the rainbow.
Seven the nails in a horse's shoe.
Hammer swing high, hammer swing low,
horse be shoed newer than new.'

And from the bag slung over her shoulder, she took out the hammer handed down from her ancestors; the hammer dedicated to Ogun, God of Iron; the hammer she never travelled without. And with a swing-high swing-low, and a little tap here and a little tap there, the horse's hooves were soon padded, polished, ready to prance.

Imagine the villagers' surprise when the black woman blacksmith returned riding the white horse and stroking its mane. Everyone had to agree that even their own Blackie couldn't have done a better job.

'As splendid a shoeing as I've ever seen,' said Blackie. 'The woman certainly knows the trade.'

'Shoeing horses ain't woman's work,' said Mr Thatcher the thatcher. 'At least, not here in Tweedham-on-Twee.'

'Wait a minute,' said Blackie. 'I'm up to my neck in work. An extra pair of hands is just what I need.'

'But there won't be room for her at the inn,' said Mr Thatcher the thatcher.

'Who said anything about the inn?' said Blackie the blacksmith. 'There's room enough in my cottage.'

And it was no use arguing with Blackie. Once he had made up his mind about anything, that was that.

And so it came to be that in the village of Tweedham-on-Twee, a white blacksmith and a black blacksmith found themselves sharing the same forge and living under the same roof.

'Two heads are better than one,' Blackie told his new workmate, as they threw nuggets of coal onto the fire.

'One head does not hold up a roof,' replied the woman, as they took turns working the bellows.

When she told him her name was Ogana, meaning 'child of iron,' he smiled and told her it was a nice name. 'Unusual,' he added. 'You won't find another with a name like that round here. I'm just plain old Bob, known to all as Blackie.'

'But you too are a child of iron,' she said, reminding him that in the beginning God came down to earth on an iron rope, and with the help of a magic hammer shaped the first humans out of metal before breathing the breath of life into them.

'If the first humans were made out of metal, now I know why some folk are still so hard-headed,' laughed Blackie. Then, as if struck by a brainwave, he said, 'Mind if I call you Blackie? With me and you – us two both being blacksmiths – Blackie and Blackie would be a laugh, don't you think?'

'Blackie and Blackie,' repeated Ogana. 'There's a certain ring to it!'

'With two blacksmiths working away under one roof, it's bound to have a certain ring. Oh, it will be ringing all right. You can count on that. Let's give nosy folk round these parts something to write home about.'

And to the jumping of sparks, the striking of hammer, the ringing of anvil, they sang as they worked well into the night:

'Swing, hammer swing.
Ring, metal ring.

Red hot white hot,
give it all you got.

Glow, iron, glow.
Blow, bellows, blow.

Be you spade, hoe
or horny hoof,

by pincer, by tong
by power of song,

we shape you
newer than new!'

The villagers did not know what to make of all this. They had always thought that Blackie was a kindly but odd fellow. Didn't Mrs Cobbler, who never missed a trick, once spy him turning his anvil upside down to ward off evil and mumbling to himself as if casting a spell?

'And now, would you believe it,' observed the same Mrs Cobbler, 'there's him not swearing and grumbling like the Blackie of old, but singing merrily with that coloured lady.'

'Sounds like our Blackie and his blacksmith lady are getting on like a house on fire,' said Mr Thatcher the thatcher.

'Peas in a pod,' said Mr Farmer the farmer.

'Flint and chalk more like,' said Mr Mason the mason.

'God sends messengers of all colours,' said Mr Parson the parson.

'But this is Tweedham-on-Twee,' said Mr Thatcher the thatcher. 'For generations, our blacksmiths have been folk from Tweedham-on-Twee. Who needs change? If it ain't broke, why fix it? Fingers crossed, she won't be stopping long. Besides, I very much doubt she'll survive a winter hereabouts.'

But she did.

Come winter, when Ogana and Blackie weren't working at the forge, or pumping the bellows, they'd be in their hobnailed boots out in the snow, having fun. Ogana even hammered out iron sliders to fit onto homemade toboggans for the children in the village. And though the villagers grumbled amongst themselves, they also knew there wasn't another blacksmith for miles and miles.

'Who would mend our pots and pans?' asked Mr Baker the baker.

'Who would shoe our horses?' asked Mr Saddler the saddler.

'Who would repair our hoes and scythes?' asked Mr Farmer the farmer.

'And what about the grates and pokers for the fireplace?' asked Mrs Miller, wife of Mr Miller the miller.

'And what about the latches for our gates?' asked Mrs Cobbler, wife of Mr Cobbler the cobbler.

They all had to agree there was no shortage of work for a blacksmith.

And one morning, after a night of stormy winds, when the villagers woke to find the weathercock toppled from its perch on their village church, even Mr Thatcher the thatcher had to admit that now, more than ever, Blackie really needed that extra pair of hands.

'We'll soon have that weathercock back on its feet,' said Ogana.

And Blackie looked at her in wonder when she told him what she had in mind. 'Shall we surprise the village with a weather-hen to keep the weathercock company? As the proverb says, "the hen also knows it is morning, though she does not crow about it".'

'Oh, a weather-hen will certainly give these folk something to crow about all right!' laughed Blackie, who couldn't wait to get started.

So into the wee hours of many a morning, their hammers rang on the anvil as they sang with one voice:

'By fire, by air,
by water, by earth.
Weathercock be repaired:
Weather-hen take birth!'

And so it happened that a weathercock and a weather-hen of splendidly wrought iron were now perched on the village church of Tweedham-on-Twee.

A handsome pair turning in the wind.

Mr Thatcher the thatcher stroked his chin and said, 'Those two Blackies have done us proud. They've made us a couple of beauties for the old church. Will take some getting used to, mind.'

And it was on a sunny June morning in that very church that Blackie the black woman blacksmith and Blackie the white blacksmith got married. Yes, Ogana, child of iron, and plain old Bob, also child of iron, were joined together by Mr Parson the parson.

Mrs Cobbler, of course, thought she must be seeing things again as the couple rode to the church on the same white horse that had once run wild in the field off the old Roman road.

Instead of exchanging wedding rings, Blackie had hammered

out for his bride an iron brooch in the shape of the sun. How it gleamed on her gown. And Ogana, child of iron, hammered out for her groom an iron pendant in the shape of a horseshoe which she threaded on fine leather. How chuffed her Bob was, to be seen wearing it.

To this day their cottage still stands in the village of Tweedham-on-Twee. The cottage with the sign that to this day says simply *Smith & Smith.*

THE GHOST OF JOHN EDMONSTONE

How lovely to return in disembodied raiment – that is to say, in ghostly form – to my beloved city of Edinburgh, an invisible presence mingling with the hurrying, fog-wrapped embodied ones. But how long these souls will be embodied – well, that remains in the hands of the Creator.

When I, John Edmonstone, was alive and teaching taxidermy to students of Edinburgh University, to be invisible would have been a big ask of my pigmentation. For in the early 1800s, I was the only black man living on Lothian Street: known to all the locals as 'the coloured gent who stuffs birds at number 37'.

During that time, my paths happened to cross with a young student, eager for private lessons in taxidermy (or bird-stuffing, if you insist). Considering how invariably skint students are, this one must not have been short of a penny or two, for he offered to pay me a guinea an hour. Not to be scoffed at.

When I agreed to give him private lessons, the young fellow thanked me with a dour manner that made him seem older than his sixteen years.

'Thank you, Mr Edmonstone. You're a gentleman and a scholar.'

If truth be told, I got the impression he was keen to skive off his medical classes, and for his first lesson he showed up with grubby fingers and fifteen minutes late. By way of apology, he explained that he'd got a little carried away rooting around the grounds of the university for any signs of worms, snails, slugs, beetles.

'The time just flew by in the jot of an eye, Mr Edmonstone. So sorry.'

I had to smile and thought to myself, Well, if you're going to be late for a taxidermy lesson, what better excuse than rooting around for creepy-crawlies? By the way, have I mentioned that his name was Charles Darwin? Strange, how the afterlife perverts one's memory, making one sometimes forget the little details of import to the earthbound.

Even then, I could sense Darwin's appetite for natural history and an omnivorous curiosity about the world around him. His was a mind brimming with questions, unshackled by that cautious English tendency of not wanting to pry, and preferring to seek easy refuge in dispassionate discussions about the weather.

'Are you from Africa, Mr Edmonstone, if you don't mind my asking? You see, I've never met a real live black gentleman before.'

It was pleasing to hear him say black. Not coloured. Not sable. Not tawny. Nor dusky. His youthful directness was so endearing, I told him proudly that I was indeed of African blood but my small-boy days had been rooted in the tropical rainforest of British Guiana in South America.

'Did you meet any tigers there?' he asked with a wide-eyed earnestness that amused me.

'Sorry to disappoint you, young man, but tigers, no. However, I did see, basking in dark creek water many a caiman

– a gigantic alligator that can pass for a floating log until it shows wide its savage teeth. Ah yes, more than once did I encounter a slithering camoudi, the snake that can constrict a body in the deathly twinkle of its embrace, not to mention furry sloths with three toes hanging from branches like upside-down philosophers, and howler monkeys that greet the morning with such a mighty howling they can be heard for miles …'

At the mention of monkeys, I noticed he perked up a bit, but he couldn't get enough of hearing about the parrots and scarlet macaws that lit up the rainforest with their fluttering bouquets of rainbow plumage. Thereupon I regaled his captive ear with tales of my adventures, going by foot through mangrove swamps, and by canoe over raging rapids and rivers, deep into the Guiana hinterland.

'Mind you, I was but a youngster when Charles Waterton took me on my first expedition,' I reminisced.

'Did you just say Charles Waterton? The explorer? I've read his *Wanderings in South America*. Inspiring stuff. Don't tell me you actually met the man himself?'

'Well, my boy, I have sat with Waterton as close as we're sitting at this very minute. One to one. Black and white. When that cursed time of humans calling humans "cargo" has turned to rust the conscience of men, it is heartening to find one uncorroded conscience. Some said he was crazy. Eccentric. But he had a heart of compassion for the trees, the birds, the animals. He respected the native people, the Amerindians, who knew the rocks, the rivers, the waterfalls, the unmapped tracks like the palms of their hands.

'Waterton would take me with him on many an expedition,

and believe me, he was the only white man I ever saw run up a tree barefoot. And it was from him I learned the skills of taxidermy. Of course, the Ancient Egyptians were ahead of us by thousands of years. Hadn't they been embalming cats, dogs and others pets to be companions in the tombs of their dead Pharaohs?'

Darwin seemed a wee bit surprised by this revelation, and there were times when I felt that perhaps I'd been rambling. Once I said to him, 'Young man, you're paying me a guinea an hour for taxidermy lessons, not to hear me reminisce. I must earn my wage.'

Eventually, we'd return to the nuts and bolts of taxidermy: Waterton's secret of preserving birds in mercury so they didn't appear like stuffed dead specimens, but an uncanny lifelike presence forever perched in its own mortality.

Again and again Darwin would ply me with questions. Once I was about to tell him that the name, Edmonstone, had in fact been the name given me by my former … I could not bring myself to utter the word 'master', for the Creator intended no one to be master of another. It was enough to say that the kindness of a white stranger had brought me to the shores of England. I refer, of course, to Charles Waterton, who was my mentor, my father figure, my friend. And whatever bird-stuffing secrets I had learned from Waterton, I wholeheartedly passed on to Darwin, this Shrewsbury teenager, whose paths would cross with mine on Lothian Street, Edinburgh.

My tuition in taxidermy seemed to have stood him in good stead when he made that famous trip on HMS *Beagle* to the Galapagos Islands. But by the time the young man had evolved his head into theories of Evolution, I was already dead. A citizen of the Great Beyond where, thank God, there is no talk of superior and inferior races.

All in all, this brief out-of-body return to earth has been worth it, for imagine my surprise to see on Lothian Street a plaque to commemorate the name of yours truly, courtesy of Edinburgh City Council. A pleasant change after centuries spent residing in footnotes. Who knows, perhaps one day I shall have the pleasure of bumping into Darwin in the Great Beyond. But I'll always think of him as that curious sixteen-year-old who, sounding older than his years, had reached out a hand and said, 'Mr Edmonstone, you're a gentleman and a scholar.'

How well I remember our conversations. Young Darwin and myself. Two wingless bi-pedals condemned to think.

LOOK! HE'S BEHIND YOU!

Out of the darkness there came a multitude who called themselves the Fig-eaters. And out of the darkness there came another multitude who called themselves the Sausage-eaters.

Under a midnight sky that billowed blue-black, they had arranged to meet on the open field that bordered their lands. There they halted, playing for time, waiting to see who would be first to speak. After an unbearable silence, the Fig-eaters and the Sausage-eaters all began chanting at the same time:

'We are the People of the Book.
We spread the truth, hook or crook.'

Such assertive certitude was not exactly the best way to break the proverbial ice towards a friendly exchange. For if the Sausage-eaters had been listening to the Fig-eaters, and vice versa, they would have realised they were both chanting exactly the same thing. Singing from the same hymn sheet, if you prefer.

Observing the proceedings from the heights of her plump golden cushion was none other than Mama Moon, known for her ever-changing moods. And tonight Mama Moon was in the mood for minding the business of bickering earthlings.

'Why not spin a coin to see who speaks first?' suggested Mama Moon.

The Fig-eaters were not keen on this idea, for in their eyes, spinning a coin was a sure sign of decadence. Coin-spinning was for those infidels – the Sausage-eaters. But Mama Moon with her luminary tongue managed to talk them into it by explaining that coin-spinning was a glittering display of what's known as democracy. Or fair play, in the words of an Englishman dressed in a white coat and famous for sticking an index finger towards the clouds.

Of course, the Sausage-eaters, who were partial to a bit of what the Fig-eaters called decadence, immediately agreed that under the circumstances, coin-spinning would be in order. So they started chanting with one voice:

'Very well. The toss we'll spin,
and may the best god win …'

The Fig-eaters decided to play along, shouting all the while:

'It's not about win or lose,
it's about paying your dues
and turning the screws
when one god calls the tune …'

At the mention of one god calling the tune, some of the Sausage-eaters took to rocking their heads and tapping their feet. A couple of white-bearded oldies (sorry, make that senior hirsute patriarchs) reached for their harps in the manner of a Hollywood Western and began bigging-up their god with riffs of psaltery.

But it was only a matter of time before the Sausage-eaters brought up a subject close to their hearts, the subject of sin. And so, lifting their voices like banners to the heavens, the Sausage-eaters cried with one voice:

'No sin too big it can't be forgiven
by a good atoning!'

And lifting their voices just as high, the Fig-eaters replied:

'No sin too big it can't be cured
by a good stoning!'

Mama Moon could feel confrontation brewing in the air but decided she'd better stay mute, for neutrality was something she'd always prided herself on.

It's true, Mama Moon had a soft spot for the tides of the ocean,
but did she not also shine her beams on earth, on tree, on mountain?

Yes, at least for now, Mama Moon would play the beaming broker. But it was clear to see that the tone of the dialogue was swiftly heading for the tone of diatribe. Raising their fists and beating their chests, the Fig-eaters hurled more words of mockery at the Sausage-eaters:

'Under your cathedral's ding-dong bell

we hear the coming of the infidel!'

The Sausage-eaters in turn started raising their fists, but instead of beating their chests, they extended their arms the way scarecrows do:

'You have some cheek!
You who doubt one God adds up to three!
You who dare to doubt the holy Trinity!'

But the Fig-eaters gave as good as they got. With a single voice they replied in kind:

'Blasphemy! Blasphemy!
One God adds up to three
equals idolatry!'

Just when the exchange seemed to be taking a mathematical turn, the Fig-eaters chimed in with:

'We Fig-eaters are the keepers of the keys.
Judgement Day will find you on your knees
begging mercy of the one God who is three.'

'"Keepers of the keys" indeed! Oh no, you're not!'

'Oh yes, we are.'
'Oh no, you're not.'

'Oh yes, *we are.*'

'Oh no, *you're not.*'

The Fig-eaters and the Sausage-eaters seemed intent on keeping up their bickering forever and ever in the manner of an exotic British tradition known as panto.

And in a moment of sheer mischief close to lunacy, Mama Moon bellowed, 'Look! He's behind you!'

'Behind us where?' screamed the Sausage-eaters.

'Pray tell us, who's behind us?' screamed the Fig-eaters.

And thinking that the voice from the heavens must mean that God was lurking somewhere behind, the Fig-eaters and the Sausage-eaters started whirling this way, whirling that way, following the bewitching omnipresent echoes of *'Look! He's behind you!'* And they whirled themselves into such a marvellous state of giddiness, they completely lost their sense of balance, with Fig-eater stumbling headlong into the arms of Sausage-eater, and Sausage-eater likewise stumbling blindly into the embrace of Fig-eater, making Mama Moon feel she was the midwife of a new dawn.

DID SOMEBODY SAY PESSIMIST?

He'd always see the tunnel at the end of the light. And he had no doubt whatsoever that behind every silver lining there looms a dark cloud.

That Italian fellow, Dante, had got it all wrong, as far as he was concerned. *The Divine Comedy* was a misnomer. He wouldn't describe this mortal coil in terms of the divine or the comic. What's so divine about being tortured through eternal circles of hell? Only those wearing the rosiest of tinted glasses would consider the paradisial pie in the sky as worth every minute of the three-score-and-ten years of torment.

The prophet after his own heart was by far Ecclesiastes (or Eccles, as he liked to call him). *Vanity of vanities; all is vanity* … Good on you, Eccles! Spot on!

Another kindred soul was that seventeenth-century Frenchman, none other than the Duc de la Rochefoucauld. With a name like that, who wouldn't feel they're in ennobled company? It was the Duke (as he liked to call him) who pointed out that 'happiness or misery are usually bestowed upon those who already have an abundance of the one or the other'.

There is nothing more comforting than the Duke, whose Maxims he keeps at his bedside for a little light reading. For the melancholic Duke was never blinded by the bubbly Parisian glitz. Now, there's a man who was happy to say publicly, 'My prevailing humour is melancholia.'

No doubt there are women out there, seeking a date in cyberspace, who stress that a sense of humour is an endearing quality in a man. But isn't a sense of humour overrated? Oh, wouldn't it be so refreshing to say honestly to a blind date over a glass of Chianti that your prevailing humour was in fact melancholia?

How even more refreshing if the date was still there for the arrival of the tiramisu.

The single life does have certain advantages, he'd agree with that. No chance of getting toothbrushes mixed up in a dimly lit bathroom, though that might be considered a trivial example.

Unfortunately, the women he's met so far online seem to be all going for a sense of humour. 'The jolly gene', so to speak. Is the compatible humour of melancholia too much to hope for? This talk about opposites attracting each other is a load of rubbish. All he wants is a soulmate. The sort of woman who sees the glass as half-empty and fancies a bit of doom and gloom. Someone uncomplicated and willing to share his shadows. The kind of woman who couldn't care less for being over the moon. The type who'd be willing to have a relationship with someone who'll be committed to reassuring her that the proverbial grass is green on *neither* side.

In him she'll be sure to find a partner always ready to lend a captive ear to every tale of woe she can produce from her baggage of the past. His will be a dependable shoulder to moan on. There's nothing like a good moan. They can have an early night-in whinge and whine. A problem shared is a problem halved. Or so they say. And not for the want of trying.

But he'll keep on searching for that special someone. Someone who'd be content just to sit with him around a candle-lit dinner. Staring at each other like a pair of scales, holding hands perhaps, watching together how sorrow outweighs joy.

KING ARTHUR AND THE SQUARE TABLE (AS TOLD BY JESTER)

All's not well in New Camelot.

Never before have I seen our King Arthur sat so rigid on his throne in the posture of Rodin's famous *Thinker*, though I'm more inclined to recall that statue by Paolozzi outside the British Library in London, where a bronzed Newton points a pair of compasses above an unsuspecting globe, as if caught in mid-motion – that is to say, as if caught (perish the thought) at the halfway point of configuring the gravity of a bowel movement.

Speaking as Jester-in-Residence, by Royal Command to the House of New Camelot, I reserve the right, by virtue of my cap and bells, to take the odd anachronistic leap of faith and folly across the span of centuries. Therefore I'm at liberty to say that right now, the King is in deep shit, or to put it less bluntly, 'Something untoward aileth the King!'

Could the reason for King Arthur's brooding by chance be the breaking news that his political advisor, trusted Merlin, having transitioned (shape-shifted, he called it) into his feminine embodiment, now prefers to be addressed as the Right Honourable Merleena, the Wizardess? Imagine the wonder of it all when Merlin appeared, not in his august blue robe, but in a shocking pink off-the-shoulder number that trailed the mosaic floor of New Camelot's corridor of power.

As official Jester, I am duty bound to report almost verbatim the conversation which transpired between Merlin – sorry, Merleena – and good King Arthur:

'My Lord, henceforth be I known as Merleena,
which I dare say more becomes my demeanour.
Merlin, I put behind me. *Passé*. Laid to rest.
Make way for Merleena the Wizardess.
Or if you prefer, my Lord, let your tongue twirl
around simple abbreviated "Merle".'

To Merlin's revelation, King Arthur, ever fair of mind, responds in a tone of voice that wavers somewhere between the somewhat astonished and the graciously Stoic:

'Ah well, you might have shifted gender,
but you'll always be Merlin the sorcerer.
Merlin no more, but Merlin no less,
though you now be Merleena the Wizardess.'

And as in the budding of his little-lad days, when seated at Merlin's knee, he'd beg a tale from the wise one's lips, so now does troubled Arthur beg of Merlin to re-tell how Uther Pendragon (Arthur's biological father) with a little help from Merlin's magic, had managed to experience an interlude of unadulterated adulterous one-to-one with a certain Lady Tintagel, wife of Lord Tintagel, the Duke of Cornwall.

'Takes me back to the good old days of yore, when your dad,

Uther Pendragon (God rest his soul) had the hots for a certain lady – Lord Tintagel's wife,' Merleena says.

'So I robed your smitten dad in Lord Tintagel's guise,
and while the old Duke of Cornwall was off fighting,
your dad (bless him) was busy having an early night in –
with the Duchess in the Duke's bed until wee dawn,
having utterly un-pent himself, that Uther Pendragon.'

Across Merleena's face there moves the shadow of a smile as she recalls Uther Pendragon's night of amorous dalliance. Since Merlin had since shaved his legendary beard as part of becoming Merleena, her smooth ruddy cheeks now remind the King of a baby's bottom. But King Arthur keeps that thought to himself.

Now, had the King requested this Jester's opinion, I would have told him, 'No big deal, Your Majesty, for when Merlin answers to Merleena, you might have lost a father figure, but gained yourself an agony aunt, in a manner of speaking.' No doubt my words would have fallen on deaf ears, for already King Arthur was fearing having to view his affection for Merlin through the fondness of a different lens. A lens as clouded as his own eye was, at this moment, threatening to become.

So, suddenly shifting the conversation to less awkward territory, King Arthur invokes the child within himself.

'Dear Merlin, pray thee, sing me if you will, a lullaby,

as you did when sleep escaped my toddler's eye.
Merlin's lullabies, I do recall, weren't exactly jocular.
Indeed, scary enough to give sleep itself the shivers.

Under Briton's mounds and hills
sleeping giants whisper still,
grinning gnomes call barrow home,
walking ghosts make their voices known
to all who liveth by the skull and bone …'

But before King Arthur could get too carried away with his own crooning, Merleena interrupts:

'How well, my Lord, do you remember those lullabies.
But have you not forgotten one important lesson?
What good is a King's manly sceptred stride,
without the precious gem of his feminine side?'

At the mention of feminine side, King Arthur can't help smiling. Then, rising from his throne, he strides across the floor, growling and beating his chest:

'Ha! My feminine side, did you say? I, the Bear?
I, who in my enemies strike pale-faced fear?
Was it by my *feminine* side, on the Mount of Badon,
that I did slaughter those Saxons invading our Briton?
Forgive me, wise Merlin, if I put to you this question:
Oh why, tell me why now, why this gender transition?'

Whereupon, for the King's benefit, Merleena gives a little twirl in the manner of a catwalk diva and tells him:

'Well, I thought, Life's far too short to be binary.
Why not, in my twilight years, try the non-binary?
Or have you not, my Lord, heard the latest tidings –
that the ladies of the realm have taken to jousting?

Forsaking the fine arts of crochet and embroidery,
they're flocking to evening classes in Archery.
In saddle seated and snorting like their horses,
see these fair ladies gallop the jousting courses,

their brazen bras like buntings flying from their lances.
I daresay, a most memorable of circumstances!
Indeed, my Lord, to this most un-ladylike ferment,
even Sir Morien has granted his endorsement.'

'Sir Morien?' repeats King Arthur. 'Valiant Sir Morien? Eloquent of tongue and none more nimble with a sword. Of Moorish birth? What more can one ask of a Moor?'

As he utters these words, King's Arthur's tongue seems to be in a spot of bother getting itself around all that tongue-twisting 'more' this and 'more' that, which made this Jester want to laugh out of his motley breeches, for I have long known the Sir Morien of whom they spoke.

But to me he was simply Moor. My best mate. My bosom companion. A man of raven skin and a smile that would put to shame the whiteness of snow.

Many a time and oft, I have sat with Gawain, Lancelot and Merlin in the company of Moor, who would regale his captive audience with tales of his homeland. Once he made us laugh when he let us know that it was his ancestors from the Land of Cush who, by their magical arts, had helped to roll the giant blue stones from the bowels of Pembrokeshire and had laboured side by side with the Ancient Druids to lay the foundation of (wait for it) Stonehenge.

'Nice one, Valiant Moor,' was all Lancelot said.

At first, I myself didn't know whether or not to take Moor seriously. I thought old Moor must be having a laugh. Or, to put it more poetically, taking the piss. We took his story with a pinch of salt and two pinches of sugar.

'Laugh,' said Moor, wrinkling eyes oceanic deep. 'But my black ancestors, believe it or not, woke Europe from their white sleep.'

'Pray, tell us more, Moor,' joked Lancelot.

By now Moor was in full flow:

'While Europe lay shrouded in her Dark Ages,
my ancestors were busy translating the pages
of ancient Sanskrit texts into Arabic, my friends.
The first to trace how through the air light bends,
which you'll find is called the curvilinear path.
I say this, gentlemen, with neither boast nor wrath,
but did we not introduce Europe to the orange, the fig,
the pomegranate, not to mention the fruits of Euclid –
that Greek who measured the dance of geometry?
So am I right or am I right? Come on, answer me.

Was it not the Arab (praise him) Al Gaber Bin Hayan,
who had mothered algebra? Why the silence, man?'

But what really made us think he'd been pulling our legs was when he confided his dream of mobilising his fellow Moors across the length and breadth of New Camelot in order to set up the first-ever Confederation of Black Morris Dancers.

Moor went on to explain that the Confederation of Black Morris Dancers would be known as COBMD – pronounced in the best possible Welsh accent. Like something out of *The Mabinogion*.

'Morris, as you guys might not know, is rooted in "Morisco" – the name for a Spanish Moor. So, my friends, how to take the Moor out of the Morisco, without severing your nose to spite your face at one blow?'

Hearing Moor speak like this of his dream of a Confederation of Black Morris Dancers, Gawain whispered to me, 'He's gone bonkers!'

Lancelot could not restrain the giggles, spilling his jar of ale. 'Have you been drinking, Moor?'

But I, Jester, can vouch that Moor had touched not a drop, not even a wee dram, for his Muslim faith forbade him to partake of what he called 'the Devil's water'. A tumbler of cranberry juice was his chosen tipple, trust me. Moor needed neither wine nor ale to loosen his tongue or set his feet whirling for the delight of noble company. Indeed, Moor has even been known to adorn his knees with tiny bells and strut his Morris dancing stuff for King and Country.

But now it was time for Merleena, in her wisdom, to put

a finger to her lips and say in her usual mysterious manner: 'Africa's seed shall take root in the flesh of Albion.'

And in the silence that followed, you could have heard a straw drop, never mind a penny or a Euro, when Moor reached across the ivory chessboard before us and took Gawain's king hostage, crying out with glee, 'Your King's kaput! Your Shah is no more, old mate. Checkmate! Shah Mat! If you'll pardon my Arabic.'

Yet, all this was banter in good faith, and that night I swear no man would leave the drinking hall with grievous harm to his anatomy.

After Merlin/Merleena had relayed to the King this unsettling chain of events, Arthur, standing full-height in the manner of a bear – he was, after all, secretly known as Arthur, the Bear-Man – exclaimed:

'Fake news! Fake news! Nothing but fake news!
I'll not have New Camelot divided by loony views!'

At that point, I, Jester, still discreetly ensconced out of earshot, leaped at the mention of loony, a word often applied to yours truly. How politically incorrect can you get! No, I'd much rather be addressed as Fool, thank you very much.

Suddenly spotting me through the corner of his cornea, King Arthur declared, 'Ah, there you are, Fool. Not spying on your King, I trust?'

'You know, my Lord, how well Fool knows his place.
And that place I do swear, my Lord, never to mis-place.'

'Ah, Fool,' sighed Arthur, 'What would I do without you?
Fondest of creatures who doth turn my grey to blue.'

Needless to say, I was pleased to hear that my immodest foolery had played a modest part in the decor of the King's mind. Thereupon I brainstormed my brain cells for the sign of a silver lining behind my grey matter. Then, out of nowhere came this brainwave. A Eureka moment! An Einstein high! A Joycean epiphany! To sum it up: a solar-powered ecologically friendly light bulb awakening.

Thus the idea of a square table had started to shape itself in the void of my mind. Had the Round Table of Old Camelot not had its day? So why not, yes, bloody why not a square table to grace the hallowed hall of New Camelot? Time for change was long overdue. The proverbial shit was about to hit the fan (no, let's keep it clean, shall we?). So I'll rephrase that. The proverbial turd was about to hit the chandelier, for no fan was anywhere in sight.

Even as we spoke, unrest was brewing. The commotion outside the castle gates was all due to a bevy of high-ranking ladies, bent on assaulting the imposing statue of no less a dignitary than Arthur's belated father, the Right Honourable Uther Pendragon.

There they were, in brazen daylight, defacing his stony face with lipstick-scrawled graffiti, vandalising his motionless person with chamber pots whose contents seemed hot off the press, in a manner of speaking, all the while howling for justice like a Greek chorus, claiming that the said Uther Pendragon had forced his patriarchal will on Yguerne, wife of Lord Tintagel.

Of course, these good ladies might well have had a point, for a paternity test would prove Arthur to be the fruit of the loins of one Uther Pendragon. Just for the record, there was no need for a maternity test to prove that Yguerne did indeed have a bun in her oven. Or, to put it more daintily, there was indeed an embryo to be named Arthur swimming in her private pool.

At this moment, King Arthur, reaching the end of his wits as well as his tether, turns and cries: 'Oh Merlin, woe is me! Whoever it was said something rots in Denmark knows well New Camelot.'

But before Merleena could say a word, and go all mystical on us, I think I'll put forward my simple pragmatic vision of a square table for the King's consideration. Something for Arthur to ponder in his mind's in-tray.

'Lend me an ear, left or right, either one will do.
Harken, Oh King, to Fool's point of view.
I say, my Lord, in the current mood of dis-solution,
may I propose a square table as the solution?'
'A square table? Like hell! Over my dead body!'
bellows King Arthur in a tone of mockery.
'Fool, have you mislaid your marbles? Get real!
That Round Table witnessed my father's royal seal.
Was it not Merlin himself who with his wizard's skill
built that table, which my dad left me in his will?
Sorry, Fool, but this is not the time for foolery.
Not when we're gripped by a crisis of identity.
Not when our ladies clad themselves in armoury,
and none can tell a jousting he from a jousting she.

Even Sir Morien, beloved Moor, urges his black kin
to deck their knees with Morris bells a-twinkling.
Of what troubles await, I've not the slightest inkling.'

At this stage of the proceedings, I, Jester, have no choice but to go for what's known as the hard-sell.

'Good on Moor!' I say. 'May his bells tinkle for evermore.
And may moreish be his days over hill, dale and moor.
But seated at square table, we'll look each other in the eye
fairly and squarely. My Lord, all I ask, is give it a try.'

Then stepping forward to my side, old Merlin, staff
in hand, puts in a good word on Fool's behalf.
'Nothing ventured, nothing gained,' says the wise one
to the King. 'Take heed, my Lord, of Fool's suggestion.'

'So be it,' says the King. 'Merlin's advice is my command.
I'll order, this instant, the squarest table in all the land.'
And so the square table is delivered forthwith.
Carved of sturdy oak. All 360 degrees of it.

But much to the King's despair, alas and alack,
the mighty package boldly states *flat-pack*.
The instructions inside are written in Norse.
No Welsh sub-titles, which makes matters worse.

And to add salt to the wound, what is required
is an odd device, known as a Phillips Screwdriver.

Once again Merlin saves the day. 'Calm down, my Lord,'
he tells the King. 'Cast your mind back to Excalibur,

that famous sword with scabbard by magic empowered.
So make thee haste, my Lord, to the Lady of the Lakes
who shall grant thy wish – one Phillips screwdriver.
Dither no longer, Sire. I say, on with your skates.

Thereupon, following Merlin's advice, King Arthur heads for the lakes. After what seems like eternity, the Lady of the Lakes appears in a barge, standing tall in a see-through gown of muslin that does justice to the rippling marble of her torso. But in the King's present hour, his distraught: 'My kingdom, my kingdom for a Phillips screwdriver!' is topmost on his agenda, and thoughts of lust kept on a leash.

So on the shores of the lake, there stands the King, eyes shielded, head bowed with courtly grace. Then, the Lady of the Lakes, hands held high like the Statue of Liberty, presents Arthur with the magical Phillips screwdriver.

Bingo!

And so in the twinkling of a screw here, a screw there,
and with much nerve-tingling anticipation in the air,
how wondrous to see that Square Table well and truly
assembled from flat-pack into its upright gleaming glory.

With the finished thing, King Arthur does seems most
content.
And of course there follows much feasting and merriment.

Old Moor needs no encouragement to take to the floor.
Gawain, his mate, blackens his face to look more like Moor.

Moor likewise whitens his face to match Gawain's
complexion.
Oh how those two knees-up and high-five in jubilation!
Across that Square Table, each face each fair and square.
With my little eye I spy Arthur's wife, Queen Guinevere,

and good Lancelot exchange smitten looks any Fool could
see,
whilst under the table their feet do play at footsy-footsy.
At head of table sits King Arthur in his most royal
composure.
Wise Merlin, in all his coiffured Merleena element of
glamour,

blesses that Square Table with both good cheer and
gravitas.
According to his foresight of what fate will come to pass,
King Arthur will one day rise again from six feet under
Cadbury's hills to restore a New Camelot world order

where love, fair play, justice shall embrace every border,
and so shall nations thrive with mindsets not tribe-bound.
I, Jester, who know my place is neither square nor round,
keep my fingers crossed and for once do silence my tongue.

CITIZEN OF THE CROSSROADS

At the crossroads of sun-hot and winter-wrapped, you see now with childhood's eye the embers of burnt cane leaf drifting in a breeze like dandelion, though back then you were a stranger to dandelion … far from the you watching now with grown-up eyes the slow downward dance of tiny snowflakes like a flurry of white fireflies without the luminescence, a descent of ghostly morsels spat out from January's mouth.

Your eyes follow the lamp-lit snow-crusted road leading to the flint-walled Saxon church in a shire of England, the church with the oval-shaped stained-glass windows, and the weathervane cockerel perched above the spire, now too frozen to crow for a denying Peter. Not like that Mr Rooster in The Tradewinds calypso song, crowing and strutting his stuff with sixteen sexy chickens chasing him. And how smoothly those sixteen sexy chickens rolled off your tongue as a child – though alliteration and assonance were furthest from your thoughts. Your small-boy tongue would marinate itself in a spicy Creole sauce, despite English Grammar ruling with a little help from a primary-school teacher's ruler smacking your small colonised knuckles.

A trans-Atlantic leap from the street lamp in front of an English pub at the corner leading you back to the bottle lamp of a coconut vendor's cart, a glowing sanctuary where coconut water is the nectar for a tropical body-hot night, cooling the throat of darkness, calling to life the storyteller, the yarn spinner, the joke-cracker …

Out of the woodwork of a wooden veranda to a turreted red-brick balcony with hanging baskets of geraniums to greet your gaze in forecast gale-force winds. But you give thanks for a short February, hoping that sooner rather than later, Wordsworth's memorised daffodils will be pouring their yellow from the upright chalices of themselves and usher an early spring to your step …

… and out on summer's patio you're set to slice an apple which you sprinkle with a pinch of salt and a dollop of pepper sauce to jazz it up as you did to a half-ripe mango in a schoolyard within hearing of Atlantic's roar and the inescapable symphony of a sea called Caribbean. And that hobbling figure on a slippery pavement, now walking a dog on this below-zero night, a walking stick in one hand, a leash in the other … could that be, by any chance, poly-lingual Papa Legba, Lord of the Crossroads, disguised in red and brown tweed, bidding you, 'Good evening,' in Received Pronunciation?

Or for that matter, Hecate, triple-faced mistress of the witch-blessed, owl-eye night, delivering three directions straight to your door-mouth, though you speak not a word of Greek?

All this while you watching, you discover the dark
continent of yourself, hearing an exodus of ancestral
footsteps echoing down the highways and byways of
inner cities, dales, downs, moors – and
just you watching you,

needing no visa or passport
to the citizenship of the crossroads.

ACKNOWLEDGEMENTS

First, apologies and thanks to Arthur Conan Doyle, creator of Sherlock Holmes, that legendary pipe-puffing crime-solver of Baker Street.

Since the hidden transatlantic history seeps into the DNA of some of these stories (and not being a historian myself), I've dipped into various sources, including *Staying Power: The History of Black People in Britain* by Peter Fryer (Pluto Press 1984); *African Presence In Early Europe* edited by Ivan Van Sertima (The Journal of African Civilizations 1985); *Black And British: A Forgotten History* by David Olusoga (Pan Books 2017); *Green Unpleasant Land* by Corinne Fowler (Peepal Tree Press Ltd 2020); *To Hell Or Barbados* by Sean O'Callaghan (Brandon: New edition 2001).

To the Australia-born lady I occasionally meet on the bus. Her name, she said, was Shiri (meaning *song of my soul* in Hebrew). Thanks for sharing your veterinary cat story. Mine is a flight of fiction.

My thanks to Peter Ayrton for his positive response to this my first collection of short stories. In this there is a certain poetic synergy for it was Peter who, back in 1984, as editor of Pluto Press, took on board *Mangoes and Bullets,* my first adult collection of poems to be published in Britain.

Thanks also to his publishing partner Rosemarie Hudson for supporting the idea and welcoming me into the HopeRoad/ Small Axes family.

Thanks to Joan Deitch for her careful copyediting and for

relating the fact that she had a chuckle, for a chuckle from your first unknown reader is music to a writer's ears. To keen-eyed Sue Cook for her comprehensive proofreading.

Also much appreciation to Yve Akehurst for typing some stories into Word document format, and to my friend Mark Hewitt for helpful feedback.

And to Grace, my poet-wife, and daughters Lesley, Yansan, Kalera, grandson Marcus, Lesley's partner Jay, for being there in the journeying and the dreaming.

John Agard, 2022